On The Z Bar 3

On The Z Bar 3

All Things

Jack Swenson

Copyright © 2010 by Jack Swenson.

Library of Congress Control Number:		2010906439
ISBN:	Hardcover	978-1-4500-9124-4
	Softcover	978-1-4500-9123-7
	Ebook	978-1-4500-9125-1

All rights reserved. No part of this book may be reproduced or transmitted in any form or by any means, electronic or mechanical, including photocopying, recording, or by any information storage and retrieval system, without permission in writing from the copyright owner.

This is a work of fiction. Names, characters, places and incidents either are the product of the author's imagination or are used fictitiously, and any resemblance to any actual persons, living or dead, events, or locales is entirely coincidental.

This book was printed in the United States of America.

To order additional copies of this book, contact:
Xlibris Corporation
1-888-795-4274
www.Xlibris.com
Orders@Xlibris.com

74619

THANKS

Thanks to my wife Sherrye for putting up with me while I write.

Thanks to my daughter Jackie who has worked with me on this book

Thanks to my grandson Jesse who's picture is on the cover.

CHAPTER ONE

Dallas Bismark Ziglar stepped off the bottom step from the deck of the main house and headed for one of the horse barns. This had to be one of the darkest days of his half-long life. Oh, the sun was shining somewhere, but here in West River, South Dakota, it was blocked out by heavy clouds. There was no chance of rain that the land needed so bad, just a gloomy grey day. What difference did it make now? It hadn't rained in the last six months, and then they only got a quarter of an inch. What hadn't dried up, the fires burnt up. The river was fifteen feet below normal and going down every day.

He was going to saddle Prairie Wind and take one last ride around the ranch before he signed the foreclosure papers tomorrow. The loan company said they would give him thirty days to get his belongings off the Z bar 3. It wouldn't take that long because everything on the ranch, except Prairie Wind and a few personal items, were in the mortgage.

He had failed. As the fifth generation on the Z bar 3, he wasn't able to hold it together. It wasn't his entire fault, he knew, but at twenty-six, he thought he had what it would take to put it back together. He had argued with his father about buying that last twenty thousand acres. The price was too high, and they were going to have to mortgage the whole ranch to do it. His dad had said, "Don't worry, son, it will rain again. It always does. The cattle prices will come back up, and we will need that extra pasture."

But it didn't rain, the pastures dried up, there was no feed for the cattle, and the cattle prices were still low.

The bank went along with them as long as they could, but they needed some kind of payment to satisfy the mother bank in Rapid City. Then came that fateful day. Dallas remembered it like it was yesterday. His mother and father had taken the Bonanza and flew out into Montana to see if they could round up some hay for the cattle. Three days later, his folks called from Miles City. They had found hay and were coming home. Dallas told them to watch the weather, cautioning them that it was overcast and there was a fog rolling up the river.

Later that day, he sat on the porch swing with a cup of coffee. It had started to drizzle, and the visibility was down to a quarter of a mile. His folks would have to turn around or maybe go into Pierre, but that was okay. He had everything under control around the ranch.

Hank, the ranch foreman, came up the steps onto the porch and plunked himself down in a chair.

"Want a cup of coffee?" asked Dallas.

"Yaw, sure."

Dallas went in the house and came out with a cup and the coffeepot. He poured Hank a cup and filled his own. He had just sat back down on the swing when he heard a plane go over the house. It was low and fast.

"That ain't your folks, you suppose?"

"I'll bet it is. I told Dad to watch the weather, but you know him—when he wants to come home, he's coming home!"

They heard it circle off to the east and around to the south. They followed the sound as it headed west and then north.

"He must have decided he didn't have enough visibility to land. They'll be calling from Pierre for us to come and pick them up. I hope he has enough altitude to clear those buttes up on the north line."

About five that evening, the FAA from Miles City called and asked if his parents were there. They said his dad had failed to close his flight plan.

Dallas was nervous. There were no phone calls, no word from his folks, nothing. The next day, it cleared, and the Civil Air Patrol was out looking. They found the wreckage that afternoon ten miles north of the ranch headquarters. There were no survivors.

Dallas climbed up on Prairie Wind and was just riding across the airstrip that hadn't been used since that fateful day. That was another thing—Dallas had wanted his dad to sell that stupid airplane. It was just one more thing they didn't need when things were so tight. If he only would have listened, they could have used the money, and he would still have his folks.

He rode to the end of the airstrip, which overlooked the Missouri River. It was wide at this point and real good fishing. He wondered what it was like when his great-great-grandfather first came to this country and saw it for the first time.

Herman was just twenty-one when he left Austin, Texas, with that small herd of cattle back in the 1870s. He heard there were grass, water, and land to be had up in the Dakota Territory. He and two of his friends took those cattle all the way north, getting here the end of July 1871. Just a little north of where the main ranch building was now, they managed to set up some corrals and dug a room back in the high bluffs along the river, covering it with poles and sod to keep out the elements. He had read and heard about all the good things of the territory, but nobody told him anything about the severe winters. That winter, he lost over half the cattle in a blinding snowstorm, and if it hadn't been for the Indians in the area, bringing him food when he was so sick, he may not have made it himself. His friends had gone back to Texas, and he was left there all alone. He was almost ready to give up himself when spring broke, and the warm days and green grass persuaded him to remain.

That summer, he met Hilda. She was a waitress/cook in a café in Pierre where he ate whenever he went in for supplies. That fall, they were married, and she moved in to the new one-room frame house he had built during that summer and fall. Over the next couple of years, they had two sons, Adolf and Ole. Herman named the ranch the Z bar 3. Z stood for *Ziglar*, and the 3 was for him and his two sons.

Herman was one of the main men working to get South Dakota statehood and on Nov. 2, 1889, he and Hilda were on the platform at the new state capitol in Pierre when the documents were signed admitting South Dakota as the fortieth state. This was the south part of the Dakota Territory. The north section was admitted the same day as the thirty-ninth state. Bismarck was chosen as its capitol.

Adolf, the oldest, never got along with his dad very well. He was a wild kid, kind of a prodigal son. He married an Indian girl, and within six months, he left her, fortunately leaving no children. He headed up to Canada with a girl he met at a bar in Bismarck. This almost broke his mother's heart, and as far as Dallas knew, he was never heard from again. Ole, the other son, stayed on and later took over the ranch.

Ole married Helga in 1905, and to this union, three children were born, Joe, who died when he was seven from the flu, Axel, and Wilma. Wilma went off to teacher training, married, and taught school up in northeast North Dakota.

Axel, stayed on the ranch and married Sara. He was a real go-getter, and during this period, the ranch grew in size to almost thirty thousand acres. After the dam was built down by Pierre, the Missouri River on the east boundary of the ranch turned into a wide lake, and the headquarters was moved to its present location. They got rain, so there was grass. The cattle prices were good after the war, and the ranch grew in both buildings and cattle.

Axel and Sara had three children, Mildred, Mary, and John. Mildred married and moved to California. Mary never married and was a missionary in Africa for many years. John chose to stay on the ranch.

John was more of a playboy than his father, and although he later took over the ranch, he wasn't as serious about it as his predecessors were. He built the airstrip about twenty-five years ago, so customers could fly into the ranch and look over the foal crop. Buyers were flying in from all over the United States to see the mighty fine horses he had for sale. It was one of these customers who, when she left, took John's heart with her. He couldn't forget about the lovely Sherrye. Six months later, Dallas's dad and mother were married.

It was during this time that they built a new ranch house and added a couple of horse barns for the fancy colts they were raising. John liked horses and did very well selling the foals that were born every year. The cattle side of the ranch grew during this time too, thanks to Hank Olson. He was probably the best ranch foreman in this part of the lower forty-eight.

Now it was up to him, and he had failed. Dallas rode on out past the hangars on the end of the runway. In one of the hangars still sat the Piper Cub that his dad used to fly around the ranch whenever there were cattle missing. Dallas soloed out in this plane when he was only fifteen years old, but he had not flown it since his parents were killed in the Bonanza.

He rode on past the hay fields that were brown and dried up into the bluff country where they pastured the cattle, on past half-dried-up ponds, around dams that he and his dad had built for water for the cattle, and on up to the top of one of the highest buttes on that part of the ranch. From here, he could see for miles in every direction. He saw a few cattle here and there, most of them hidden from sight behind a hill or down in a ravine. He was going to miss the ranch, and he didn't know what was in store for him, but one thing he did know was that God said in his Word in Romans 8:28, "And we know that all things work together for good to them that love God." He believed this! Why did he believe it? First of all, he had always believed it. Now it came down to the fact that this was the only thing he had left to believe in.

He circled back to the east until he came to the river and followed it north. As he rode along, a speedboat on the river passed him going upriver, probably loaded with fisherman heading for the boat landing farther up river on the east side. Ever since the Lake Oahe Project Dam was put in, the river had good fishing, and fisherman came from all over the Dakotas and Minnesota to try their luck. He passed between the Missouri and the Homestead on up about half a mile to the original place where his great-great-grandfather first built. It wasn't the exact spot—that was underwater because of the river rising after the dam went in. Now the river was so low you could almost see the original site. There was the old one-room house and small barn. This wasn't the original one that Herman built, but Dallas and his dad had built it as close to the original one as they could. It had been a lot of fun and kept the history of the ranch alive in their minds. It was also fun to show visitors who came to the ranch.

He stopped at the cemetery where all of his ancestors were buried. He got down off of his horse and walked by each gravestone. He was going to have to leave this all behind, probably never to see them again. He remounted and pushed on farther north, finally stopping on the top of another butte to eat the lunch that Martha had sent with him.

It was going to be hard to tell Hank and Martha and the few cowhands that were left on the ranch that he had lost it, and they would have to find other work. Hank and Martha had been there ever since he could remember and were more like family than they were foremen. When his folks were killed, Martha started cooking for Dallas, and before long, she and Hank just moved in the big house. It was a big happy family. Most of the cowhands had been on the ranch for several years, and then he had let the late-comers go when things got tough and money got short. He sure didn't want to do that because they had about the same amount of stock, but everybody dug in and somehow they managed to get all the work done.

He sat there on the ground overlooking the ranch to the south, eating a fried chicken drumstick. Martha was never satisfied to just send a sandwich or two. No, she had to send fried chicken. There was even a piece of cherry pie in the lunch, which he had eaten first.

Hank and Martha never had any children of their own and had always treated Dallas just like he was theirs. He always got birthday and Christmas presents, and now since his folks were gone, he was theirs.

This was all his, he pondered as he took in the sight of the ranch from the top of the world, at least for a few more days. He had done his best, and there was no more that he could do. When the cattle prices went down, what little money came in he had to buy feed for the cattle because without rain, there was no grass on the entire ranch. Then came the sick and dying cattle and the prairie fires. It was more than he could handle. He even had to sell some of the horses and cattle to buy feed for the rest of the herd. There was no money to pay the mortgage on that twenty thousand acres they hadn't needed in the first place. He thought of that verse in Proverbs 3:5-6, "Trust in the Lord with all thine heart and lean not on thine own understanding. In all thy ways acknowledge him and he will direct thy path." He sure didn't know what God had planned for him, but he was still going to trust him.

Off to the east and as far as he could see to the south, the Missouri River glistened in the noonday sun. It was beautiful. To the west, far in the distance, he could see the main gate to the ranch with its stone pillars and steel wagon wheel gates. He looked north up past the high buttes. It was all the Z bar 3, and it was his. Next week it would belong to someone else. He had failed.

CHAPTER TWO

Dallas sat on the high butte overlooking the ranch and thought about the day six months ago that it had dawned on him that things were really getting rough.

It was a hot windy day in West River country, and Dallas Ziglar was tired. He had been in the saddle all day checking cattle and repairing a fence here and there. Several of the watering holes were almost dried up, and there was no rain in the forecast. He had stopped watching the weather on TV. That was a waste of time, and besides, it was depressing. It had been almost six months now since they'd had a rain that did any good. They really didn't need much rain. The area averaged only four to five inches a year, and if they got that much, they had all kinds of grass. The watering ponds would fill up behind the dams his father and grandfather built years ago. It wasn't only him and his ranch but the whole country that was dry. The Chinook winds out of the hill country took what little moisture there was in the soil. They wouldn't get a hay crop this year, and they got very little last year. He had already sold some of the cattle and used the money to buy hay for the rest of the herd. That couldn't go on forever. Hay had to be trucked all the way from Montana or Minnesota, and it was getting very expensive.

As he came up out of one of the draws, he saw Hank, the ranch foreman, and another man working on one of the line fences. He rode over to see how they were coming.

"How's it going, boys?" he hollered when he got within earshot. They turned around and watched him ride up.

"It's a funny deal, Dallas," said Hank. "It looks like this fence was cut."

"What makes you think that?"

"Well, take a look." Dallas climbed down off his horse.

"You're right. It was cut."

"This is the third one we've found today."

"None of the cattle have gotten out. In fact, there aren't any tracks even close. But take a look over here. It appears to be horse tracks of a single rider."

"Now who in the world would go to all the work of riding out here and cutting the fence? For what reason?"

"Beats me," said Hank. "We're gonna keep heading down the south line before we call it a day. When you get back to the ranch, let Martha know we'll probably be late and not to wait supper for us. I'll just warm up some leftovers or somethin'. I don't know how many more cuts we may find. The horse tracks came from the south and rode right up the fence line. We just hit the tracks back about two miles."

"I'll follow this fence up to the main road on my way back to the ranch. See you guys later," said Dallas as he rode off to the north. He passed the places that Hank and Jim had already patched and kept going north. By the time he reached the main road into the ranch, he had stopped and fixed a couple more cuts. The horse tracks turned and went out toward the main gate.

Dallas was puzzled. They had never had any trouble with the neighbors, at least not in the last few years. He remembered his dad telling the story about his great-grandfather who caught one of the neighbors stealing cattle. He just took some of the ranch hands and went over to the guy's place, took him out, and hung him from the nearest oak tree. But that was back before the turn of the century when this country was the Wild West. They had good neighbors now. If they needed any help, all they had to do was call. There were good people living around here, and there wasn't anybody that he didn't trust.

He had just turned down the main road heading for the ranch headquarters when he heard a vehicle approaching from behind. He looked back to see a white Cadillac coming up behind him. He moved out of the middle of the road as the car pulled to a stop beside him.

"Is this the road to the Z bar 3?"

"Yes, it is. Who are you looking for?"

"We're looking for Mr. Ziglar."

"What for?"

"Well, cowboy, I guess that isn't any of your business."

"What if I make it my business?"

Dallas got down off his horse and walked around to the front of the car. He took a pen out of his shirt pocket and wrote the license number down on his hand.

"What are you doing?"

"I'm writing down your number so I know who to charge with trespassing when I call the sheriff."

"Well, young man, I don't know who you are, and for that matter, I don't care, but I am going to report you to Mr. Ziglar."

"Just what would you like to report? I'm Mr. Ziglar."

"I'll report how you treated us to your father."

"That may be kind of hard. He's been dead for over two years."

"You mean you're the only Ziglar, and you're the boss?"

"That seems to be right."

"Well, I'm sorry. I thought you were just some smart-aleck cowboy."

"We don't have any smart-aleck cowboys on this ranch."

"I apologize for the way I spoke to you. I'm Mr. Bill."

"Frankly, I don't care who you are. I suggest you just back down that driveway to the main road and get out of the country. Don't try and turn that boat around 'cause if you get off the drive just a little bit, I'll have you arrested for trespassing."

"But we have a business deal for you that's too good to pass up."

"I don't do business with men who treat people like you do. Now get moving," said Dallas as he climbed back in the saddle and laid his hand on his 30-30 Winchester. He watched as they backed down the mile-long drive, out through the main gate, onto the road, and head back the way they came.

When he got back to the house, he would called the sheriff and have him run the license number to see who those guys were. For some reason, he didn't have a very good feeling about them. He sure didn't like their attitude. He told Martha that Hank had said it would be late before he got back and not to wait supper. She said she would make something for him and put it in the fridge.

"I'll leave a note on the table, and then I'm going to bed. I'm tired."

Dallas was still up reading when Hank came in.

"Found several more cuts in the fence," he said.

"I wonder what's going on. It seems that someone's trying to make life miserable for us."

"Well, we got things put back together again, but we'll have to keep our eyes open."

"Martha said she left something for you to eat in the fridge. I'm going to get some shut-eye," said Dallas "We'll take care of it in the morning."

Several days later, Dallas was doing some paperwork in the office. This was the job he liked the least. He would much rather be out on the range somewhere doing anything but paperwork. There was a knock on the door, and Martha stuck her head in.

"There are a couple of guys here to see you, Dallas," she said.

"Send them in."

Dallas looked up as the two men walked into the office.

"Well, good morning, Jim, what brings you out on such a nice day?" he said as he stood up behind his desk and stretched out his hand to shake hands with the banker.

"Good to see you, Dallas. I would like you to meet Mr. Gustoffson from our mother bank in Rapid City."

"Mr. Gustoffson, this is Dallas Ziglar, owner of the Z bar 3."

They shook hands and Dallas said, "Have a chair, gentlemen. What can I do for you?"

Jim Parker, the president of the bank where Dallas did business, looked over at Mr. Gustoffson and then spoke. "Dallas," he started, "Mr. Gustoffson here has been asking me about the loan you have on the twenty thousand acres your father bought a couple years back. I know things are real tough in the ranching business right now, but you haven't made any payment on the principal the last few months. Now don't get me wrong." And he held up his hand. "We know that you've been through some real bad things with your parents being killed and all, but we were just wondering what your plans are?"

"Jim, I don't really know. With no rain and the cattle prices being down, it's hard enough to buy hay and make the interest payment. I guess I don't see how I can make any big payment on the principal right away."

"Have you given any thought to selling the ranch?" asked Gustoffson.

"No, not really, this ranch has been in the family for over a hundred years, and I plan on making it another hundred."

"There's a real-estate company in town that says they have a buyer for this ranch if you would want to sell it," Gustoffson continued. "You might give it some thought because we will expect you to start paying on the principle very soon. I think we're finished here," said Gustoffson as he stood up. He put out his hand to Dallas and said, "I hope to hear from you soon." He turned and headed for the door. Jim came over to shake Dallas's hand, and said under his breath, "I'll do what I can."

That night, Dallas didn't sleep very well. What was he going to do? He was just barely able to buy feed for the cattle and pay his men. Now they wanted him to start paying on the principal for the twenty thousand acres. Maybe he would have to think about selling at least part of the ranch. But with land prices as low as they were now, he wasn't sure that would even help.

He prayed, "It's your land, Lord, your ranch, and your cattle. What are we going to do about it?" He went to sleep and dreamed that somebody was trying to steal the ranch from him.

CHAPTER THREE

Miss Shay Everhart rolled down the gravel road in the West River country of South Dakota. It was a beautiful day, and she had the top down on her red Mustang convertible. Her strawberry-blond hair blew in the warm afternoon breeze. *What a nice day to be out in God's country, whoever that was.* She didn't know much about God, and she didn't think about him much, nor did she really care.

She was a Texas girl, just out of college, working for the Jippem Real Estate Co. in Rapids City. Why she left Texas to go to school at the University of Minnesota in Minneapolis, she really didn't know. It seemed like the thing to do at the time, and after four years, she graduated with a degree in business. Her girl friend persuaded her to come to Rapids City and go to work for the same company she was going to work for. After a few months with the Jippem Company, she realized that this may be something that would work for her. Oh, she didn't want to work for anyone else, but at least she was getting some experience in the land business, and soon she would set up her own shop.

She liked the sales end of the business, and her friend and coworker said the only reason she was so good at it was she was so darn good-looking. The women even liked her, and the men were a pushover. Twenty-four years old, five foot four, hundred fifteen pounds, and a figure that said she should be in Hollywood.

Her friend said, "I can sum it up in one word—you're beautiful. Really, you should be in the theater."

"I know it said, 'Shay selling popcorn,'" and she grinned at her friend.

"How do you ever expect to get a man with that attitude?"

"I don't want a man. When I get my business set up and running, then and only then will I think about a man."

"I know. You weren't any fun in college either. You always had your nose in the books while all the men went crazy."

"Most of the men you hung out with were crazy to start with."

Her mission today was to find the Z bar 3 Ranch and try to buy it. She wasn't sure who the buyer was, but her boss said he had a cash client if she could make the deal. He said the ranch owners were having a tough time with the lack of rain and the cattle prices down. They were behind on their mortgage payments and may or may not want to sell.

Was this the right road she was on? She wasn't really sure. It had been a long time since she left the village of Tumble Weed. The sign on the edge of town said, "Population 48." It wasn't much of a town. A bar and grill, gas station/convenience store, and a church were all there was on Main Street. There were a couple of houses behind the general store and a few more on the road leading out of town. She had stopped and filled her gas tank, paying fifty cents more a gallon than in Rapids City.

It had been a while since she had even seen any buildings in the distance or a road leading to a ranch. Up ahead, stopped in the middle of the road was a pickup, and she could see a cowboy off to the side working on the fence.

She pulled up behind the pickup and stopped. The cowboy, who was working down in the ditch, finished what he was doing, picked up his tools, and started toward his truck. Shay got out of her car, and as she walked around the front, the breeze played with her skirt, adding an extra touch to her already beautiful appearance.

"Howdy," said the cowboy as he approached.

"Can you tell me how much farther it is to the Z bar 3?"

"You're here," he answered.

"I'm on the ranch?"

"Yep."

"Where can I find the owner? I'm sorry. I'm Shay Everhart." And she put out her hand.

"James Wilson," said the cowboy.

"Probably, at headquarters," said Dallas. "What do you want him for?"

"I just need to talk to him."

"Where do I find the headquarters?"

"Go back about two miles to the crossroad, turn left—you must have missed the sign. It is easy to miss. It is only twenty-four feet long," he said with a big grin.

"I might have. I was so busy looking at this beautiful country."

"You have to pay more attention. The traffic is really bad out here." And again he grinned at her.

"What do you mean? You are the first person I've seen in the last half hour."

"Well, it gets really bad at rush hour. You must not be from around these parts?"

"No, I'm from Rapids City."

"That's a good place to be from, a long ways from," Dallas added.

"So when I get to the crossroad, where do I go from there?"

"Turn left for a couple of miles, and you will come to the main entrance, stone pillars with iron wagon wheel gates. Over the road is a big sign, "Z bar 3 Ranch." Of course, you might miss it if you missed the sign at the crossroad. If you do miss the road, go down twelve miles, turn around, and stop on your way back." He grinned.

"You won't let me forget not seeing the sign, will you?" she said.

"Not if I can help it."

"Thanks, do you work for the Z bar 3?"

"Sometimes."

"Where can I turn around?" she asked.

"Just turn around in the middle of the road. I'll stop the traffic." And he smiled again.

"You don't take life too serious, do you?"

"You might just as well enjoy it. You won't get out of it alive anyway."

"Would you turn my car around for me? I'm afraid I'll run in the ditch."

"I don't know if I can drive a fancy car like that," Dallas said.

He got in and easily turned it around. When he got out, he held the door open while Shay got in.

"Like your cowboy boots," he said as he looked at her high heels. "Work pretty good, do they?" *Nice legs too,* he thought to himself. *Don't see many women as pretty as she out in the back country.* One of these days, he was going to have to find one for himself.

She didn't answer as she drove off toward the crossroad. When she got there, sure enough, there was the sign, bigger than her car. How in the world did she miss it? No wonder the cowboy was so smart about it.

If all the men in this country were as good-looking as that one, maybe this would be a good place to live. He was a handsome one all right, six foot four and built like a quarterback, long wavy brown hair sticking out from under his hat, bright blue eyes that twinkled when he teased her. Probably in his mid—to late twenties with a tan that said he had spent a lot of time in the sun. She guessed he must be single 'cause he wasn't wearing a ring.

She turned south and, before she knew it, came to the main gate. Shay turned in, admiring the entrance. About a mile east of the gate, she topped a small hill, and there before her lay the pettiest ranch she had ever seen. Straight ahead of her was a mammoth house or lodge or something. It was beautiful, right out of a Western movie. Hand-split shingles on the roof with several dormers. Rough-sawn siding and a lot of heavy timbers supporting the covered porch on two sides of the house. Off to the left and farther back were a couple of smaller houses and a bunkhouse, and to the right were several barns, corrals, etc. Behind the building, she could see the Missouri River. It was beautiful. She could see why somebody would want to buy this place.

She parked in front of the main house and walked up the flower-lined brick walk. In front of her were wooden log steps that led up to a long covered porch. On her left was a porch swing, and on the other side were a couple of benches and deck chairs.

She crossed the plank deck up to heavy wooden double doors and knocked. While she waited, she looked of to the east and the wide Missouri River. *Man, what a sight. Nobody would sell this beautiful place unless they had to. If they were to sell it, they would want a lot more than Mr. Jippem said to offer them for it.*

She was about to knock again when the door creaked open. There stood an attractive middle-aged lady drying her hands on a kitchen towel. If it weren't for the grey streaks in her hair, she could pass for late forties. "Good afternoon, may I help you?" she asked in a pleasant voice and a smile on her face.

"Yes, I'm Shay Everhart. Is Mr. Ziglar in?"

"Yes, he is. I heard him come in just a few minutes ago. You're in luck. He's very hard to find in the daytime. Follow me."

She stepped into the great room and stopped in awe. Right before her was a massive stone fireplace. Above the heavy log mantel was a picture of an old cowboy, probably one of the founders or something. Around the perimeter of the room was a balcony with a log railing and a log spiral stairway leading to the second floor. She could see closed doors probably to bedrooms. Three groups of sofas and overstuffed chairs were arranged around the room. Several small tables and lamps completed the arrangement. From the ceiling in the center of the room hung a heavy wagon wheel chandelier.

The sound of her name brought her out of the trance she was in. "What a beautiful room," she said as she hurried to catch up to her host.

On the right side of the room, they stopped in front of a closed door with a sign that read "The Buck Stops Here."

Her host knocked.

"Come in," called a cheery voice.

"Ms. Everhart is here to see you, Dallas." She turned to Shay. "Go on in, miss," said her host.

As Shay stepped in, her mouth dropped open as she looked at the man behind the desk.

"I'm Dallas Ziglar," he said as he extended his hand.

"Shay Everhart," she stammered.

"Yes, I know, twenty-six years old, five foot six inches, one hundred and twenty pounds, blond hair and blue eyes. You live at 1437 Emerson and work for Jippem Real Estate," he said as he looked at the computer screen. "No criminal records—oh, oh, two speeding tickets in the last six months." And he looked up at her.

"You're Dallas Ziglar?" she asked with a bewildered look on her face.

"Yep," he said as he turned the nameplate on his desk around and looked at it, "that's what the sign says."

"But you told me when I first met you out along the road your name was James Wilson."

"I am Dallas James Wilson Ziglar. My mother got carried away with the names. Most of the time, I just go by Dallas Z., except when there is a lovely lady around. Then sometimes I get all nervous and mixed up." And he grinned at her.

She just stood and starred at him. She was flustered.

"If you are selling magazines, insurance, windows, siding, want to find me a wife, or want to sell my ranch, I am not interested and don't have time to talk. If not, I am all yours."

She still didn't say anything.

"Hello, Earth calling Shay."

"You don't play fair. I came to talk to your father. You have been teasing me since the minute I met you. I need to talk to the boss."

"I'm sorry. He was killed in a plane crash two years ago."

"Oh, I'm sorry. Then is your mother in charge?"

"My mother was killed at the same time as my father."

"But who is the lady who answered the door?"

"Oh, that's Martha, my housekeeper."

"So you are the boss?"

"Yes, ma'am, I'm all there is. I'll have to do."

"I am so sorry for the loss of your parents." And she put her hand up to her forehead as her face turned red. "I have made such a fool of myself. Can we start all over again?"

"Sure"—and Dallas put out his hand—"hello, I'm Dallas Z."

She looked at him in disbelief and then stood up and took his hand. "I'm Shay Everhart."

They shook hands, but Dallas didn't let go. He held her hand as he looked into her deep blue eyes. "They sent a beautiful blond to help me change my mind, didn't they?"

"Excuse me?" answered Shay.

"You are the third one they have sent to help me sell my ranch, and I sent them all packing. Now they send the most beautiful girl in all of South Dakota to do a job three men couldn't do. Well, it won't work. The only reason I didn't tell you to leave when I first met you out on the north road is because you are so very attractive, and we don't see very many pretty ladies out in this part of the country. I am sorry that I teased you and led you along. I apologize. Now if you'll excuse me, I'm very busy." And he let go of her hand and started for the door.

Shay didn't move.

"Is there something more I can do for you?" he asked.

"I didn't come all the way out here to take no for an answer. Could I take you out for dinner, and we could talk?"

"Well, I suppose you could. Maybe Souix Falls? That is a hundred sixty-three miles. Are you going to bring me back home?"

"Isn't there something closer?"

"Well, I guess we could go into Jake's, which is only thirty-eight miles, but you'll have to be prepared for every cowboy in the place to undress you in his mind as you walk in. Do you want that, pretty lady?"

"What kind of country is this anyway?"

"This is cow country. Some of these guys haven't seen a woman in months, say, nothing about one that looks as good as you do."

"Is that what you are doing, undressing me in your mind?"

"No, I have more respect than that for you. Besides, the Bible says, 'To look on a woman to lust after her. You have already committed adultery with her in your heart.'"

"Oh, you're one of those goody good, religious guys."

"No, I am just a regular guy whom the Lord has changed, and I respect women."

"Would you let me have just a few minutes of your time and let me explain what I can do for you? Please just listen to what I have to say."

"Okay, if you want to ride along, I have to go down to the medicine bowl and check on some cows." *That will stop her,* he thought to himself. *She is a city girl and probably afraid of horses.*

"How long does that give me?" she asked.

He looked at her with surprise. "Couple of hours, maybe three or four, depending on what we find."

"Okay, I'll take you up on it."

"Have you ever ridden a horse before?"

"How hard can it be?" Shay said without answering his question.

"I'll see if Martha can find you some jeans to wear. That skirt and heels aren't what you would call riding clothes."

Dallas left the room, and pretty soon, Martha came in. "Come with me, miss. We'll get you something to wear."

"Please call me Shay."

"Shay, that is such a pretty name," said Martha.

Martha led Shay into one of the bedrooms on the main floor. Again Shay was taken in by what a wonderful house this was. The walls and ceiling were of wood, making the room so Western, warm, and cozy. There were two log beds with patchwork quilts and pillow covers. A large window overlooked the prairie to the north, and it was beautiful.

Martha opened up one of the closets and said, "We keep some extra clothes in case one of our visitors wants to ride."

"Do you have a lot of visitors?"

"We used to before Sherrye was killed. She liked people. Let's see now. You are about a 6?"

"Why, thank you, let's try an 8 or 10."

"Here's a pair of jeans and a shirt. If those don't fit or you don't like them, pick out something here in the closet. I'll go and find you a pair of boots and a hat. The bathroom is right through that door. You will find clean towels on the rack. I'll be right back." And she left the room.

Shay looked around the room as she changed clothes. *What a wonderful place this is.* She was going to be ashamed to offer Dallas what Mr. Jippem said to offer him. The price was way to low. It was like fifty cents on a dollar, maybe even forty. She would surely like to live in a place like this, and Martha and Dallas, there was something different about them. She couldn't put her finger on it. Maybe it was just that they were so friendly and just nice people. Oh, Dallas was always teasing her, but she liked it.

About that time, Martha came back in the bedroom. "Wow," she said, "that fits you so nice. Here, try on these boots and this hat.

"You look like a cowgirl, but can you ride?"

"Dallas asked me the same question, but I didn't answer him. I did barrels in high school rodeo. That has been a few years ago, but I think I will be okay."

Martha laughed. "This is good. I noticed Dallas was having a lot of fun at your expense. Now it is your turn to call his bluff. He will put you on a very slow horse because he wouldn't want you to get hurt, but ask him if you can ride the black mare in the corral. Her name is Midnight. She is a good horse but still has a little life left in her. We'll see what he does."

As they came into the kitchen where Dallas was having a cup of coffee and a sandwich, he looked at Shay and said, "You change into a country girl quite nicely," as he looked her up and down. Her jeans fit really nice, and her shirt still showed she was a woman.

"How about a cup of coffee and something to eat before we go? It will be a couple of hours before we are back. That's if you can stay in the saddle that long."

Just before they left the house, Dallas turned to Martha and said, "We will be having a guest for dinner." And he looked at Shay.

"No, I can't—"

"Nonsense," said Martha, "I will have dinner ready when you get back from your ride. I get tired of cooking for Hank and Dallas. It will be nice to have some woman company for a change."

They left the house and headed for one of the corrals just as Hank came out of the barn.

"Hank, I would like you to meet Shay Everhart. Shay this is Hank, Martha's better half."

"Good to meet you, ma'am." And Hank tipped his hat.

"Would you saddle old Lazy for Ms. Shay?" Dallas asked Hank.

"Sure." And he turned toward the corral.

"How about that black one over there?" Shay pointed.

"Oh, that's Midnight. She's really frisky. Have you ridden before?"

"A couple of times," said Shay.

"Hank, saddle Midnight." Dallas smiled to himself.

"Really?"

"That's what the lady wants."

When Hank came leading the horse back, Dallas said to Shay, "Here, grab the saddle horn and put your left foot in the stirrup and swing up into the saddle. I'll hold Midnight until you are ready." He then thought to himself, *I shouldn't be letting her ride this horse. This mare hasn't been ridden for a month, and it will be just like dynamite. These city people think they know everything. If she lands in the dirt, she lands in the dirt.*

Shay slipped into the saddle with ease and reached for the reins that Dallas was holding.

"Are you sure you are ready?" he asked.

"Yes, just let go."

Hank stood there shaking his head, and Martha stood back fifty feet or so. Midnight took a couple of steps forward and then reared up on her back legs. Shay said, "Easy, girl," as she patted the mare on the neck. When the horse came back down, Shay gently kicked Midnight in the ribs, and she started trotting around the corral. She came back around to where Dallas and Hank were standing with their mouths open and made a quick turn, and she kicked her again and went into a gallop a couple of rounds and slid to a stop in front of the two men. "Nice horse. She rides smooth."

Martha started clapping in the background.

Shay looked at Dallas and said, "You going to walk, or are you going to get a horse?"

"You've ridden before," said Dallas as he stared at her.

"Nope, first time." She grinned.

She looked over at Martha, and Martha gave her a thumbs-up.

As the two of them rode out of the corral, Dallas looked at Shay and said, "I guess I owe you an apology for the bad time I have given you. I was sure that Midnight was going to dump you, and I was going to have a good laugh at your expense. Where did you learn to ride like that?"

"I was in high school rodeo back in Texas, but that was a long time ago."

"Why did you pick Midnight out all of the horses that were in the corral?"

"Martha told me to."

"Oh, so I was set up? You haven't been here two hours and already you are turning my people against me. What kind of a woman are you anyway?"

"You'll never know."

They crossed the ribbon creek bridge, and on they went down the bank of the wide Missouri, on and on, neither one of them saying much, just enjoying the ride.

"Are you ready to listen to me?" asked Shay.

"No, why would I want to sell this beautiful place?"

"It is worth a lot of money."

"Yes, a lot more than the other guys offered me, but then what would I do with the money? What would all my ranch hands do? Where would Hank and Martha go? Where would I go?"

"You could find a wife and travel, and do what you want."

"I'm doing what I want right now, and I don't want a wife."

"Don't you ever want to get married?"

"Yes, someday, but I want to marry my best friend."

"Have you got somebody in mind?"

"Isn't that kind of personal?"

"Yes, I guess it is, but do you?"

"No."

"But you owe a couple of million dollars on this ranch."

"The Lord will provide."

"What's he going to do, write you a check?"

They had stopped on a high ridge overlooking the Missouri. Dallas looked at Shay while the wind played with her blond hair. *My, she's beautiful,* he thought to himself. "If he has to," he replied.

"Do you really believe that?"

"Sure, he does it all the time, not giving me money, but he has given me so much more. When my folks were killed, he gave me the strength to go on. I had a bad heart when I was a kid and the doctors wanted to operate, but my mother said, 'Let's wait a couple of weeks.' My mother and dad spent almost all of the next two weeks praying for me that the Lord would heal me, and they believed he would. Two weeks later, when we went in for the operation, my folks made the doctors run the tests again. This time, they could find nothing wrong. The Lord had healed me. I have had many checkups since, and my heart is perfect. Don't you think if he can do that, he can come up with a few dollars?"

"How do you know that the doctors just didn't make a mistake in their diagnosis?"

"No, when I was a small boy, I couldn't play baseball or run or do anything—my heart would hurt so bad. We had the best doctors at the Mayo Clinic, not just one but a whole team of them. They said it was nothing but miraculous."

"I have never run into a guy like you. Most guys if they had a girl out in the wilderness all by themselves would try to make a pass at them. But you, you are telling me how good the Lord is to you."

"I'm not most guys. You are safe with me. Not because you are not attractive but because of Jesus in my life."

She looked at him and didn't say anything. She could tell he loved this land, and that he loved the Lord—whatever that meant. He was so handsome sitting there in the saddle, looking over the rolling hills of the West River. How come she had never run across a guy like this before? The guys she knew only wanted to party and chase skirts. This guy had a quality about him that she had never seen before. Did it have something to do with this Jesus? She knew people that went to church at least sometimes, and they were no different from anybody else.

"Now let's get this straight. Was I trying to sell to you, or were you trying to sell to me? I don't think I have been doing a very good job," said Shay.

"Look, see those two deer that just came down to drink out of the river?"

"Yes, and there's another one." Shay pointed down the riverbank. "They are so beautiful."

"Getting back to what I wanted to talk to you about, what would it take to get you to sell this place?" she asked.

Dallas thought for a minute. "Let me ask you a question. If it was your ranch and you lived here, would you sell it?"

"That's not a fair question."

He didn't say anything but kept looking at Shay.

Finally she said as she looked off across the prairie, "I guess if I was in your shoes, I wouldn't want to sell it either."

"I didn't ask if you were in my shoes. I asked what would you do?"

"Dallas,"—she looked him in the eye and didn't say anymore for a minute—"I wouldn't sell either." She turned and started slowly riding back toward the ranch.

Dallas galloped after her, and when he caught her, he reached out and took her arm. "Stop" he said. She stopped. "I didn't mean to upset you."

"What am I going to tell my boss when I get back? He expected me to come back with a listing from you. He has this guy who wants to buy your ranch. He has the cash in hand."

Dallas still had his hand on her arm, and he didn't move it. "Tell him that you ran into this ornery guy who wouldn't sell and threw you off his property."

"But that's not true."

"Well then, tell him you met the handsome boss of the Z bar 3 who treated you like a queen, and you fell madly in love with him, and you told him he would be stupid to sell the ranch to anyone."

"Don't you think you should put in there that he was fun to be with and teased me all the time and that I out rode him on his own horse, and that he didn't even make a pass at me?"

"Yeah, that's good. Add that in there too."

"You are no help. I'm glad I'm not trying to sell you a car. I would probably end up buying one from you."

A shot rang out! And then another.

"What was that?"

They turned and listen in the direction of the sound.

"My guess is somebody poaching deer." But that is not what he thought. "Let's go and see if we can find anything."

They topped the next hill, and far in the distance, they saw a lone rider, galloping off.

"I'll call the game warden in the morning, and let him know what we saw." They started back for the ranch again. "We better hurry. I told Martha we would be back by six, and I don't want to be late. She works hard to put on a good meal, and the least I can do is be there when it is ready."

"You are different from most men. My dad would come home for dinner whenever he felt like it, and Mother best have it ready," said Shay.

They trotted side by side. Dallas was amazed how smooth she was in the saddle.

They took care of the horses and walked into the kitchen about quarter to six. Hank was sitting at the table, having a cup of coffee. "Get cleaned up, you two. Supper will be ready in about ten minutes."

Dallas washed up and was sitting at the table with Hank when Shay came back in. She had changed back into her dress, fixed her hair, and put on some makeup and earrings.

"Wow, you look nice," said Dallas as he got up. "I better help the lady with her chair."

"See," said Martha, "you haven't been here a day, and already you are turning Dallas into a gentleman." They all laughed.

"I think I will keep you around. Maybe you can teach Hank a thing or two."

"Yes, but I already have a wife. I'm not looking for one like Dallas is. You'd think he would want to get married before he is on Social Security."

"I was just trying to show the lady there are a few gentlemen out in this part of the country."

Martha sat down and reached out and took one of Hank's hands and reached for one of Shay's with her other hand. Hank took Dallas's hand and Dallas took Shay's other hand. Shay looked around, not knowing what to expect. Everybody bowed their heads while Hank asked the blessing. Shay was surprised but felt at ease. This was something new to her, but just the feel of Dallas hand was good.

"Martha, you outdid yourself. This is a wonderful meal. I hope you don't go to this much work every night just for these two," said Shay as she took the potatoes that Dallas handed to her.

"Here, here, girl, don't give her any ideas. This is what we expect every night. Isn't that right, Dallas?" said Hank.

"Yes, it sure is."

"Now I can see why you aren't married. It seems you have high expectations of a wife." Shay smiled at Dallas.

"Well, that is one of the questions on the application I have any woman fill out who is interested."

"So how many applications do you have so far?"

"Well, I don't have any yet, but I expect them to start pouring in soon."

They finished off the meal with some apple pie and coffee.

"If I eat one more bit," said Shay, "I think I will burst." She looked at her watch. "Oh my, it's eight thirty. I better get on the road."

"We have a nice guest room," said Martha. "Why don't you stay overnight?"

"No, I better not."

"Yes, you will," said Dallas. "I don't want you out on these back roads after dark. What if you had trouble."

"Oh, I have a cell phone."

"That's right. You are a city girl. How many bars do you have?"

She took out her phone and looked at it. "None."

"I rest my case."

CHAPTER FOUR

"Okay, I'll get my bag out of the car. I always carry one just in case I get stuck out in some motel somewhere."

"I'll walk out with you so the wolves don't get you," Dallas replied.

"Do you have wolves around here?"

"Yes," said Hank, "I saw one back in seventy-three. You're being conned, girl, by this big brave cowboy or wolf."

Shay said, "Good night, you two," as Hank and Martha left the kitchen and went hand in hand down the hall to their apartment.

"What a great couple," said Shay. "They seem to be so much in love. Will you be that much in love when you get to be their age?"

"I hope to be," he said, "that is, if I can find the right woman to start with."

Shay dropped the subject and said to Dallas, "I hope I didn't tire you out too much with that ride." She grinned.

As Hank watched Shay and Dallas walk out the door from the hall window, he looked at Martha with a smile on his face. "Love is in the air, dear."

"Oh, Hank, he is just being nice to her, treating her like a guy should."

"Woman, you're blind."

The moon was coming up out of the Missouri, spreading diamonds on the water as it came.

"Oh, Dallas, look at that moon. Isn't it beautiful?"

"Not as beautiful as some things around here."

She looked up at him and drank in his eyes but didn't answer him.

"Scenes like this make me think of what Louis Toothman wrote back in the sixties, 'To love and appreciate the Rocky Mountains, you only open your eyes, but to love and appreciate the prairie, you must open your soul.'"

"That's beautiful," said Shay.

"Isn't it strange how some people can look at the moon over this wonderful land and still not believe in God the creator? We won't be able to see it tonight because the moon is so bright, but on a moonless night when it's really dark, there are a billion stars. You have to get away from the haze and lights of the city to really see them.

"How much did you say you were willing to pay me for a view like this?"

"You know we have a lot of ranches in Texas, but I was raised in Houston. I've never seen anything like this before in my life."

"If a guy could only bottle this and sell it, you could make a fortune."

"Maybe that's what I should be selling instead of trying to get you to sell your land."

"Do you really work for Jippem, or are you a model that he hired to entice me?"

"No, I really work for him, but thank you for thinking I was a model. I can tell I have to learn more about what I am trying to get somebody to sell. I would be ashamed to offer you what he wanted me to offer you. He was trying to steal the ranch from you."

He grabbed her bags out of the backseat.

"Do you think I need to put the top up in case it rains?" she asked.

"If that will help it rain, you better leave it down."

"Do you ever get any rain?"

"You've heard of Noah and the flood, haven't you?"

"Yes."

"Well, we got two inches that time."

Shay laughed. "You see humor in everything, don't you?"

"You might as well laugh about it. You can't do anything about it anyway." As they walked up on the porch, Dallas said, "Would you like to sit in the swing for a while and watch the moon rise? It's way too early to go to bed. I know you city girls are used to running around all hours of the night."

"Sure, why not? It's such a nice evening."

He set her bags down and held the swing while Shay sat down. The moon was almost all of the way up out of the river and was full, big, and bright yellow.

They sat for several minutes without speaking before Shay broke the silence. "Is it always this quiet out here?"

"No, if you really listen, it's not quiet at all. Do you hear that? Those are frogs croaking down along the river. You hear that? That's coyotes over by the west line baying at the moon. And that kind of muttering, that's some of the cattle arguing over who's going to sleep where. Listen to that chirping. That's a cricket down in Martha's flowerbed."

"But that's all quiet. I don't hear any sirens or traffic or trains or televisions blaring. It's so peaceful."

"Can you put a price on that?" Dallas asked. Several more minutes passed as they just sat there swinging back and forth.

"How long has the ranch been in your family?" asked Shay.

Dallas told her some of the history and then asked, "And what about you? Where did you come from?"

"I was born and raised in Houston, Texas. My dad is in real estate, and my mom was a stay-at-home mother. After I left to go to college, she went back to the hospital as a nurse just to keep busy. But why am I telling you all this? In the first place, you don't care, and the second place, after tomorrow I'll never see you again."

"Why? Don't you like it out here?"

"Well, yes, but why would I come back?"

"To see me of course," said Dallas.

"Why would I want to see you?" she said as she put her hand on his knee and felt the electricity go through her.

"Now you hurt my feelings."

"I'm sorry. I see you can hand it out, but you can't take it." And she slapped his leg.

"Oh, you were just handing it out? You really do want to come back and see me?"

"Well, I might if I was asked. When I go back and tell Jippem that I didn't make the sale, I'll be out of a job and have a lot of extra time on my hands."

"I'm sorry. I don't want to get you fired. Tell him I am thinking about it."

"Yes, but that would be a lie. You aren't thinking about it."

"Just tell him you made a lot of progress with me, and you think I am coming your way."

"That would be a lie too."

"No, it wouldn't. I am coming your way." He laid his hand on hers.

She pulled her hand away. "Is this where you're supposed to try and kiss me? It took you a while, but you're no different than any other man," she stormed as she stood up.

"Ms. Everhart!" He was so forceful she stopped dead in her tracks, "Don't flatter yourself. If and when I ever decided to kiss you, it will be because I love you and not before. I am pretty fussy who I give my kisses to, and don't you forget it. I'm kind of saving them for the woman I marry." He picked up her bags and carried them into the house and up the winding stairway to the balcony overlooking the great room below. Across the room and out through the massive glass wall was the Missouri not more than a quarter of a mile away. Shay stood in awe of the view that was before her as Dallas stood holding her two bags and watched. He pushed the latch of the door to her room with his knee, and the door opened. She followed him inside.

Again Shay stood in disbelief as she looked at her surroundings. The walls were of logs, and the ceiling was vaulted of rough-sawn cedar. There were two queen-size beds with patchwork quilts, and a desk-dresser combination stood along one wall. On the wall at the head of the beds were large Western pictures, one of a cowboy driving a herd of cattle and the other of two riders heading off into the sunset.

Mr. Z. brought her out of her daze by saying, "The bathroom is in here." And again she was amazed. It was nicer than any motel bath she had ever been in.

"If you need any extra towels or anything else, just let Martha or myself know. The TV is hanging on the wall above the dresser, and we have satellite, so you'll get a couple hundred channels. We may be West River, but we are up to date on technology. Breakfast is at seven. Anything else I can get for you?"

Shay just stood drinking in the room. Finally she blurted out, "I don't believe this. This is the most wonderful motel or bed-and-breakfast or whatever you are running I have ever been in. What do you get for a room like this?"

"Oh, we don't charge. Mom just liked to treat people nice when they came to the ranch. She had Dad build three rooms like this. We've had lots of missionaries, big-time preachers, representatives, and senators stay here. We've even had the governors from both North and South Dakotas spend the night with us."

"No, really, what do you get for this room?"

"Nothing. Mom never charged, and neither will I."

"Well, I'm going to pay. A room like this in Rapid City would go for two hundred twenty—five dollars a night."

"No, this room is free. If you want to pay, you have to sleep in either the bunkhouse with the guys or the barn." He walked out. "Have a good night's rest," he said as he went.

"Mr. Ziglar, I'm sorry about what I said about the kiss. I admire a man like you."

"Thank you," he said as he took her hand and kissed it.

"Does that count as a kiss?" she asked.

"No, that's a good-night kiss. When I give you a love kiss, you'll know it. It will knock your socks off." And he was gone.

As she got ready for bed, she thought to herself that maybe this ranch life wasn't so bad, but she wished that this man didn't have her so confused. She just couldn't understand him, and neither could she forget him. She had only known him for a few hours, but it seemed a lot longer than that. She had come to the ranch to talk him into selling, and now she didn't think he should. What was she going to tell her boss when she got back? She would probably get fired, but then she wasn't sure that she cared. She snuggled down under the comforter, and before she knew it, she was sleeping.

The next morning, she awoke with a start as she looked around the room. Where was she? Oh, yes, now she remembered. She was at the Z bar 3 Ranch. The sun was just coming up over the hills on the other side of the Missouri, and she looked at the clock—five thirty. It was six fifteen when she quietly closed the door behind her and tiptoed down the stairs with a bag in each hand. She made her way toward the front door. She would leave the house before anyone else was up and be on her way, never to see them again. This was such a beautiful place, and they had been so good to her that she hated to leave without saying good-ye, but it would be much easier this way.

"Good morning, sleepyhead."

She stopped like she had been shot. Whirling around, she saw Dallas sitting at the kitchen counter, drinking a cup of coffee.

"Where are you going?"

"I was just going to get on the road early," she stammered.

"Do you mean you were going to leave without even saying good-bye?"

She didn't answer.

"Sit down and at least have a cup of coffee with me before you go."

She set her bags down by the door and walked back to the counter and sat down on one of the stools.

"Nobody leaves here without breakfast. Martha would shoot me," he said as he set a cup of coffee in front of her and poured himself another cup. "Cream or sugar?" he asked.

"No, black is fine. What are you reading?" she asked as she pointed to the book that was lying in front of him.

"John."

"Just *John*? That's the name of the book?"

"No, the Gospel of John in the Bible."

"Oh." And she didn't know what else to say.

"Have you ever read the Bible?" he asked.

"I started to once, but it didn't make much sense, so I quit."

"I'll bet you started at the beginning."

"Sure, where should I start?"

"Start with John and go both ways."

"Why is that? I always start reading a book at the first chapter."

"Well, the first part of the Bible, the Old Testament, is mostly Jewish history and prophecy, which is kind of hard to understand. The New Testament is the life of Jesus and the history of the early church."

"Maybe I should try it again and read it like you're telling me to."

"Here, let me give you a Living Bible. This is in modern English." He reached behind him and took a book off the shelf. He opened it to the book of John and said, "Start reading here."

"I will," she promised, and their hands touched for a moment as she took the Bible from him.

"My, are you two up already? I better get some breakfast going," Martha said as she walked into the kitchen.

"No, that's okay. Coffee is enough for me," said Shay

"That may be so, but I know it's not enough for Dallas. If I don't feed him, he'll complain all day," she said with a grin. "Besides, Ms. Everhart, I want to take good care of you too. You see, we don't have many beautiful women come to see Dallas. I've been trying to find him a wife, but he's awfully picky and he needs a lot of care. His mother was way too good to him."

"Martha! Shouldn't you be cooking instead of talking?"

"See what I mean?"

Shay looked at Dallas. His face was turning red.

"Don't pay any attention to Martha," he said. "She's just trying to get rid of me, but I'm not really looking for a wife."

"There he goes again. If he's ever going to get married, I'll have to find a girl for him. He's handsome, a good worker, fun to be with—"

"Martha! That's enough! Ms. Everhart is probably already taken. I'm sure she's not interested."

"If she's taken, she should wear her rings," Martha replied.

"Please call me Shay, and no, I am not taken, and who says I'm not interested?" She looked at Dallas.

"Will you just feed me so I can get to work? You two are ganging up on me. What's wrong with a guy just playing the field?"

"Playing the field?" said Martha. "You're not even in the game. In fact, you don't even go as a spectator."

Shay laughed. "This is good."

"She's worse than having another mother, but I'm going to keep her."

About that time, Hank came in. "Is she giving you a hard time again?" he said as he patted his wife on the behind.

"Yes, she thinks I need a wife."

"Well," said Hank, "I've always said it's better to have loved and lost than wed and be forever bossed."

Dallas and Shay laughed.

"Sit down and eat," said Martha as she put the food on the table.

They waited until Martha sat down and Hank reached over and took Martha's hand in his left and Dallas's in his right. Martha reached over and took Shay's hand and smiled at her. Shay looked at Dallas. Their eyes locked, and he took her hand in his as he said, "Let's say Grace." And he bowed his head.

"Dear Lord," Dallas started, "we thank you for another beautiful day in which we can serve you. We also thank you for the food we are about to partake of, and bless Martha for such a good job she does for us. Be with our friend and visitor, Ms. Everhart, I mean Shay, you can call her Shay too, Lord"—Shay looked up at Dallas, and he was dead serious. He wasn't making fun of her. He was talking to God just like he was a personal friend of his.—"who is with us here today. Protect her as she travels back to Rapid. Be with Hank and myself as we work this day. Amen." And he squeezed Shay's hand before he let go.

"You guys sure do love each other, don't you?" said Shay, and as Dallas looked at her, he noticed a tear in her eye.

After breakfast, Shay said, "I must be going. I've imposed on you good people long enough."

"No, no," said Martha, "it was fun having you here. Please come back and soon."

She shook hands with Hank and Dallas and gave Martha a big hug.

"Here, let me carry those bags out for you. I don't want you telling people we didn't treat you right."

"There's not much chance of that. You've treated me like royalty."

Dallas put her bags in the backseat and said, "I apologize for Martha ribbing you about me getting married."

"Oh, she was just having a good time at your expense. I thought it was kind of funny."

"She likes to do that, but I'm not looking for a wife."

"That makes me feel bad. When you do start looking, let me know." And she put her hand on his arm and grinned.

"Will I see you again?" he asked.

There was a tear in her eye as she answered, "I guess not."

"Why?"

She looked at him as she took her hand off of his arm. "I don't know. You have me so confused. I came out here to steal your ranch from you, and you knew it, but yet you and Martha were so kind to me. You treated me like long-lost family. You fed me and gave me a wonderful room to sleep in, and somehow, I feel dirty knowing what I came here to do to you. I just want to sneak off and never see any of you again."

"And you could live with yourself if you did that?" he asked.

"Oh, Dallas, I don't know." And she opened the car door and got in. She arranged her skirt around her pretty legs and then reached up and put her hand on his arm. "Can I please just go before Martha and Hank come out? I don't know if I can face them anymore. I'm sorry, Dallas. I never meant to hurt you." She started the Mustang and put it in drive.

"I don't mind you trying to steal my ranch," he said, "but you had no right to mess with my heart." He turned and walked back to the house.

Dallas stood on the porch and watched her drive out of the yard in her red Mustang convertible. What was it about that woman that made him uneasy? She was so beautiful and intelligent and had a great personality. What a shame she didn't know the Lord. He watched her drive over the last hill. He watched until the dust settled. She was gone.

As Shay drove the two miles down the lane to the main gate, she thought what was it about this country that would make a city girl like herself enjoy it. She always thought as she drove down the interstate going east of Rapid City what a barren and godforsaken country this was. Here, she was enjoying the short time she had been at the Z bar 3 and, for the first time, saw its beauty and life. Seven miles down the main road, she came to another sign, "YOU ARE NOW LEAVING THE Z bar 3 RANCH."

There was a sense of loss. Would she ever return?

CHAPTER FIVE

As she drove down the gravel road toward Tumble Weed, she could hardly see the road through the tears that were rolling down her face. She was sobbing and made no effort to control it. She had miserably failed at the mission her boss had trusted her to complete. It wasn't all her fault. She wasn't told the whole story. She wasn't aware there had been three people before her trying to get Mr. Ziglar to sell his ranch. She just bet it was Al and Barry, two of the best salesmen in the office who had been there first, and then she was sent to try and persuade Mr. Ziglar with her womanly charm. Now she knew why Mr. Jippem insisted she where a skirt and heels. Why else would she go into cow country dressed that way?

She didn't know this ranch had been in the family for over one hundred years. It wasn't just a beautiful place along the Missouri where you could raise some cattle, hoping to make a meager living. This was a place where generations of Ziglars were born, lived, and died. Now Mr. Ziglar, who had just buried his parents on the land, was not about to move on to greener pastures. This was his land, his ranch, and his space in time to control and prolong the Ziglar name and kingdom. It was his charge and he took it seriously. He would do everything in his power to accomplish it. Sure times were hard right now, but this wasn't the first time they had been, and they lived through it. She felt she had been sent out to steal the ranch, not buy it. Oh, she had a check for one hundred thousand dollars in her attaché case for the earnest money. Now that she had been to the ranch, it seemed like a small price to pay as a down payment on a man's dream and soul.

Even though she was sent to buy from a man who didn't want to sell, he had treated her like a queen. She rode with him over the hills and along the banks of the Missouri River. She had eaten with him, his foreman, and housekeeper, one of the best steaks and meals she had ever eaten. Then he demanded she stay overnight because he didn't want her to drive the seventy-five miles of lonely country roads back to the interstate when it was dark. He had been worried about her safety. They had sat in the porch swing and talked far into the night just like old friends. She felt comfortable with him. It was just like she had come home to people she knew and loved. How could this be with people she had just met? There was something very different about them, and the attitude they had. When they prayed together around the dinner table, there was love that flowed from one to another.

He wasn't only a cowboy, but he was a gentleman as well. His men all loved him and would do anything he asked. They didn't work for him. They worked with him. He was the king of a kingdom and the land that he loved. He was handsome but not proud. He was strong but gentle. He was serious but fun loving. He was a tease, but he liked to be teased himself. He was a real He-man, but he was religious. He loved his god. That was something more than any other man she had ever known. Why were these things going through her mind? She had left him and his land behind and would never see either again. But Martha had said to come back and soon. Would she dare?

It was early afternoon when Shay walked into her condo. It was more drab and bland than it had been three days ago when she left it. The cold eggshell walls screamed for some color and the warmth of wood. The contemporary furniture just didn't come up to the standard after sleeping in the log frame bed under the cozy comforter in the room she had last night. She thought about sitting in front of the big stone fireplace with the log mantel and feeling the warmth the fire gave off as she watched the flames slowly lick up the wood. She wished she had never gone to the Z bar 3 if she was going to compare everything to it from now on. She had only been there one time and then only for a few hours and most likely would never go back. Martha had asked her to come, but what was she going to use for an excuse? Why hadn't he asked her to come?

Just forget it, she told herself. *Read a couple of Westerns and get it out of your system.*

She used the rest of the day to catch up on some housework and e-mailed some of her college friends. That night as she crawled into bed, she again compared it to the bed she had slept in last night. *There I go again,* she said to herself. *I was happy with things as they were a couple of days ago. Nothing here has changed. What is wrong with me? He wasn't interested in me, and I sure am not interested in him. What would I do with a man that all he wants to do is read the Bible and talk about God? I wonder if there really is a god. Besides, he said he wasn't looking for a wife. If he was, there must be some women on the other ranches around that would fit into his lifestyle although the ranch life wouldn't be so bad. It sure was quiet and peaceful on the Z bar 3. What am I doing? I was only with him a few hours and now I am thinking about moving to the ranch. What a dreamer. Remember, I am going to get my real estate business up and going before I even think about getting married.*

She finally drifted off to sleep and was troubled with the dreams of a cowboy who was riding off to the west. She went after him, but for some reason or other, she couldn't quite catch him. She rode hard, but he was still out of reach. It was no use. He was gone. She woke the next morning tired from being on horseback all night, chasing a man she couldn't catch and didn't know what she would do with him if she had. Now she had to get up and go to the office and explain to Mr. Jippem why she had failed. Life just wasn't fair.

She took her time showering and getting dressed, all the time thinking of what she was going to tell the boss. She tried to eat some breakfast, but it just wasn't the same as the breakfast on the Z bar 3. She even tried praying over it, but she didn't know what to say or how to do it. In fact she couldn't remember ever praying in her whole life. Finally she could wait no longer, so she got in her Mustang and drove the half mile to the office. The morning wasn't as clear or crisp as in the West River country, but this was her home, so what difference did it make? This is where she lived. *Get over it,* she told herself.

She got out of her car and walked into the office of Jippem Real Estate. The bounce was gone out of her step, and the enthusiasm she usually had for work was gone. This place was a dump. It could use some paint, and the shrubs that lined the walk needed water and some tender, loving care. She had never noticed how bad it was before. When she got her own office, that was one thing she would do. Make the place inviting and look like it was a prosperous business. Why would anyone want to buy from a firm who couldn't keep their own place in first-class condition?

Mr. Jippem was by her side even before she could get to her office. There he stood in all his obnoxious glory, five foot six inches and two hundred fifty pounds of whole blubber with most of it held in by his belt. His dingy white shirt strained to keep from blowing a button. His long stringy hair was held in place by enough grease to lubricate a Mack truck, and the two-inch cigar that graced the corner of his lips wasn't lit.

"Oh, Shay, honey, did you get me a deal?"

Shay didn't answer but walked right past him down the hall to her office, and he followed. She walked in behind her desk, and when she turned around, there was fire in her eyes. "First of all, I'm not your honey, and second, no, I didn't get you a deal."

"But a—"

"But nothing. You didn't tell me how beautiful the place was or how nice the people were. You didn't tell me he didn't want to sell. You didn't tell me you had already sent three guys out there before me to try and buy the ranch, and you didn't tell me you were trying to steal it, not buy it!" She was so mad her face was getting redder by the minute, and she was shaking.

"Shay, Shay, calm down," Jippem said as he reached behind him and kicked the door closed. "Quit screaming at me. Do you want the whole office to hear you? I sent you out there because I was sure you could get the job done."

"No, you sent me because you knew Dallas was a single guy, and he might do business with a sexy woman."

Mr. Jippem pulled back a chair from the front of the desk and sat down. Shay stood and looked down at him for a few seconds, and then she sat down too. Another minute passed, and finally Jippem said in a low voice, "What do you think we could do to put this deal together? The buyer is very anxious to buy the Z bar 3, and he has the cash ready to do it, cash mind you. Do you have any idea what the commission will be on this sale?"

"This guy does not want to sell. The ranch has been in the family for over one hundred years, and I don't think he would sell for any price."

"Everybody has a price," stated Jippem.

"I can see why somebody would want it. It is the most beautiful place I've ever been. Didn't you think so?"

"I don't know. I've never been there. I've flown over it. That's all. They don't want the buildings anyway, and they'll probably tear them all down."

"Why, that's crazy! If they're going to do that, why don't they just buy a bare piece of land somewhere? The state is full of them."

"They want at least thirty thousand acres right on the river. There aren't very many ranches that are in one piece. Besides, this ranch has a tarred airstrip that can handle small jets."

"Have you been in some of the buildings?" asked Jippem.

"Yes, I have. I was in a couple of the barns and the house. I stayed there overnight, and I ate a couple of meals with them."

"I don't know if you know this, but he may not have any say as to whether he's going to sell the ranch or not. He has a big mortgage on the property. His dad bought twenty thousand acres just before he was killed. I know the note is due, and I don't think he's able to pay it with the cattle prices being down and the fact that we haven't had any rain. Who knows? He may have other troubles in the near future. Maybe he can be persuaded to sell."

"Troubles like what?"

"Who knows? There are a lot of things that can go wrong on a ranch that size. So you're on pretty good terms with them? Did you put on your womanly charm and get that young guy wrapped around your finger?"

"Well, I don't know if you could say that. But they were very nice to me."

"Okay, this is what I would like you to do. I'd like you to make one more try at getting him to sell. Wine him and dine him. Turn on your lovely charm. This is a big deal, and the commissions for both you and me are big, real big. Do whatever you have to do. Sleep with him if you have to. That should make him happy. Then you can come back and sleep with me, and that will increase your commission even more." He grinned.

Shay jumped up, grabbed a dictionary that was lying on her desk, and hit him on the side of the head. Before he could get up out of his chair, she hit him three more times while he tried to protect himself with his arms. He finally got up and out the door, and Shay followed him down the hall, beating him all the way. All of the time, she was screaming, "I'll turn you in for sexual harassment! I'll send you to jail for a long time, you big fat overgrown sex pervert!" As he went in the door of his office, she kicked him in the rear with her pointed high heel. The door slammed shut, and there was silence. All of a sudden applause broke out from every doorway up and down the hall.

"Attagirl, Shay, he's had that coming for a long time. Good girl," echoed up and down the hall as she stomped back to her office too angry to answer any of her coworkers. Within half an hour, she had her desk cleaned out, and all her personal possessions in her car. She had cooled down enough to say good-bye to most everybody in the office before she left.

Now she was home in her cold, drab condo without a friend or a job all because of a stupid ranch and a handsome cowboy. Why should she care if he sells his dumb land or not or if he loses it to the bank for that matter? It was none of her business and no skin off her nose. But she couldn't forget about it. She just couldn't let it go. She had really enjoyed the short time she was there. Martha and Hank were such great people. Oh, yes, even Dallas. He was just too handsome, kind, and gentle for his own good, and he didn't even know it. Besides, he didn't care about her. He just enjoyed having somebody different to tease, but the whole bunch had such inner peace. What was it? He didn't really make any difference to her? She just didn't like anyone being taken advantage of, and she felt that's what was happening here. She didn't know what it was, but something just wasn't kosher with this whole deal.

She wasn't sad about quitting her job. She should have quit that slime ball a long time ago. The only reason she was working there in the first place was to learn the business so she could open her own shop. She liked the real estate business, and she was good at it. Someday, but not right now. Right now she had a mystery to solve.

CHAPTER SIX

Shay didn't sleep very well again that night. It wasn't because she had quit her job and wouldn't have a paycheck coming in. She really didn't need the money. It was the experience that she was working for. The reason she didn't sleep was farther east. She couldn't keep from thinking of the Z bar 3. What was going on out there? Why were Jippem's buyers so intent on buying that ranch? What did they have in mind? Why were they going to tear down all of the buildings? What were their plans? So many questions were running through her head that she couldn't think straight. What really puzzled her was why she was so interested. She kept telling herself she just didn't like someone being taken advantage of, but she had never gotten involved with any other cause. She didn't like high taxes, politics, government waste, or the fact that there were homeless people, and she hated abortion, but she had never gotten involved in any of these causes. Why this?

It wasn't that she felt sorry for the people on the Z bar 3. She didn't even know them. Oh, she had met Dallas, Martha, and Hank, but she didn't really know them. They were at peace with themselves. She supposed Dallas would say he was at peace with God, whatever that meant. He had a big loan hanging over his head, but yet he was at peace. So what was it?

The next day when the alarm went off, she got up and started getting ready for work. She looked at the clock. She was running late. She grabbed her car keys off the counter and was half way out the door when it dawned on her that she no longer had a job—she had quit yesterday.

Since she was already dressed to go out in public, she decided to go down to Perkins's and have a good breakfast. After that, she had no idea what she would do. She drank a cup of coffee and looked at the morning paper while she was waiting for her food to come, and when it did, she took her time eating. She kind of enjoyed this, but she knew she would soon get tired of not having a reason to get up in the morning. She was a workaholic and had to have something going all the time.

It had only been a couple of days since she was out to the Z bar 3. If she could just put it out of her mind, she knew it would be easier in a couple of weeks. *I wonder what Martha has fixed for breakfast this morning?* Whatever it was she knew it was better than what she was eating. Why did she miss Martha's breakfast? She wasn't even a breakfast person. Maybe it wasn't the food but the conversation she knew was going on around the table, and she missed it.

The waitress came to take her dirty dishes and poured her another cup of coffee. Shay took out her cell phone and dialed Sue Hogan, her college roommate who worked just down the hall from Shay's old office.

"Jippem Real Estate, how may I direct your call?" said Karen, the receptionist.

Shay hesitated for a second or two and, then disguising her voice, said, "Sue Hogan please."

"Just a moment."

"Good morning, this is Sue Hogan."

"Sue, it's me."

"Shay?"

"Shush, I don't want anybody to know I am calling. Are you free for a minute or two?"

"Sure."

"What's going on in the office since I left?"

"You wouldn't believe it. Several of the girls are going to sign on with you if you file a sexual harassment suit against Mr. Jippem, and I'm one of them. He is such a creep to work for. The only reason any of us stay is because of the money."

"Have you heard anything about the Z bar 3?"

"Yeah, he put Barry on it."

"Do you have any idea who the buyer is that Jippem has interested in the ranch?"

"No, I don't, but the word around the office is it's a cash deal and a big plum for whoever makes the deal."

"Sue, there's something funny going on with that deal. It's just that ranch and they want it bad. Jippem suggested I sleep with Mr. Ziglar just to get the job done."

"You're kidding! Did he say that?"

"Yes! That was the reason I was so mad when I quit, then he said I could sleep with him just to make my commission bigger."

"Oh, he is such a slime ball! I'll keep my ears and eyes open and see if I can find out who the buyer is."

"Don't let anybody know that you're talking to me. Somehow I'm going to find out what's going on," said Shay. "There's something crooked with this deal."

"I have to run, Shay, but I'll be in touch, bye." She hung up.

Shay knew that she could trust Sue. They had been friends all four years in college, and besides, she needed somebody on the inside at the Jippem Real Estate empire.

She thought it would be easier to forget about the Z bar 3 after a couple of weeks, but now it was all she thought about. She ran background checks on Jippem and some of the main people that were in the office. Everybody but Jippem and Barry Killmee seemed to be clean, but both of those guys had very shady pasts. Although she worked very hard the last several days trying to find out what was going on; she wasn't any farther ahead now than she was two weeks ago.

She wanted to go out to the ranch and talk to Dallas to see if he had any ideas, but then she was afraid he would tell her to mind her own business and leave the ranch business up to him. He had asked if he would ever see her again, but then he didn't say that he wanted to. Martha asked her to come back too, but she was only an employee, so Shay didn't really have a reason to go back there. She was thinking about this and trying to type a letter to her mother all at the same time. There was a knock on her condo door.

Who could that be? She didn't have very many visitors. Could it be Jippem or maybe Barry? Had they caught on to what she was trying to do? Another knock. She went to the door and peered out through the eye spy.

No, it couldn't be! She looked again. It was. Looking herself up and down and checking her hair in the mirror by the door, she wasn't at all pleased with what she had on, baggy sweat pants and an oversized sweatshirt.

Why didn't he call if he was coming over? She really didn't want him to see her looking this way.

He knocked again. She couldn't wait any longer, so she unlocked the door, opened it, and stared at the stranger.

"Hello, Shay."

"What are you doing here?"

"I came to see you."

"Why?"

"You didn't come back to the ranch, so I came looking for you. I called your office, and they said you were no longer employed there. Then I came here."

"How did you know where I lived?"

"You can find out just about anything on the Internet."

"You should have called. I look terrible."

"Okay then, I've seen you at your worst, and I still think you are beautiful."

"You're such a liar. Christians don't do that, do they?"

"No, they shouldn't, but I'm not lying."

"I'm sorry. Won't you come in?" She held the door open. "Have a seat. Can I get you a cup of coffee or a Coke or something?"

"No, I'm fine," he said and he sat down on the sofa. "How have you been, Shay? I misjudged you. I really thought you would come back out to the ranch and try to convince me to sell. How come you didn't?"

"Because I no longer work for Jippem, and besides, I changed my mind. You know a girl can do that. I no longer think you should sell. You have way to nice a place, and it's been in the family too long for you not to fight to keep it."

"Did you get fired for not coming back with the contract?"

"No, I quit."

"Why."

Shay's face started turning red, and she said, "You don't want to know."

"Yes, I do, or I wouldn't have asked."

She didn't answer for a bit but just sat there and looked at the floor. Finally she looked up at him and said, "Mr. Jippem wanted me to go back out one more time and get the deal. He said even if I had to sleep with you to get it."

"Was the thought of sleeping with me so bad that you quit your job?" he asked with a grin on his face.

"No, I mean . . . I'm not that kind of girl. I mean . . . that wouldn't get you to change your mind. I mean . . . Oh, forget it." She dropped her eyes from his.

"Shay, I was teasing. I know you aren't that kind of girl."

"How do you know?"

"The Internet! No, I'm sorry. Here I go teasing you again. I think I have a pretty good judgment of people, and you rank real high with me."

Shay looked at him again and said, "It wasn't the fact he wanted me to sleep with you that I quit, but then he said if I came back with the deal, I could sleep with him and raise my commission."

"He said that?" Dallas was instantly mad, "Why, that pig!"

"Why? What's the difference if I sleep with him or you?"

"Because I'm a much nicer guy." He grinned.

"I don't know why I am discussing with you who I sleep with. It is none of your business. When the time comes for that, I sure won't ask your permission," said Shay. "Really, what are you doing here?"

"I told you, I came looking for you."

"But why?"

"Because I missed you."

"Why?"

"Because you are beautiful, attractive, charming, lovely, sexy, alluring, gorgeous, magnificent, elegant—"

"Enough with the adjectives. Besides all that, why are you here?"

He spoke with out a smile, "I came for fun."

"What kind of fun?" she asked.

"Shay, besides all the things I said, you are just fun to be with, and I missed you," he said and he reached out and touched her arm. "I've thought about nothing else but you since the day you were at the ranch. Sometimes it gets lonely out there, and you brightened my day when you were there. I'm not here courting or anything. I just want your friendship."

"Really, I was hoping for a lot more than just friendship. Now I am sounding just like you, teasing all the time."

"That's one of the things I like about you. You can give it back when I tease you."

"Can I be honest with you, Dallas? You drove me nuts after I left the ranch. That place was all I thought about. I wanted to go back so bad. I even started out that way once and turned around because I wasn't sure you would be happy to see me."

He took her hands in both of his and held them. Their eyes met. "Will you be my friend?" he asked.

"How much does it pay? I'm sorry. Yes, I want to be your friend."

"Let me buy you some lunch before I have to leave, and we can talk."

"Okay, but let me change into something nicer." She got up and went into the other room. When she came out, he whistled. "Wow you look nice. How can you change from a cowgirl into an elegant lady in just a matter of a few seconds?"

"Like it?" she asked as she twirled around in the middle of the room. She was wearing a red skirt and white blouse with high heels to match.

"You didn't have to get all dressed up."

"If I am going out with a handsome man, I want to look at least halfway nice. I don't want any other woman taking you away from me," she replied, and she held out her hand. "Where are we going?"

"I don't know. This is your town. You tell me."

"How hungry are you?"

"Pretty hungry," said Dallas, "I didn't bother to stop for breakfast this morning."

"You mean you got away from the ranch without Martha feeding you?"

"I told her to sleep in this morning because I was leaving early and that I would stop and have something to eat on the way. I was so anxious to see you I didn't take the time to eat."

"Why didn't you call and let me know you were coming. At least I could have had on something better than sweats."

"I was afraid if you knew I was on my way, you wouldn't be here when I got here."

She looked at him for a minute without saying anything. Then she said, "Just down the street is a nice steak house. I know you like steak. It won't be as good as the ones on the Z bar 3, but it will be the best one in this town."

"How do you know I like steak?"

"Martha told me."

"What else did Martha tell you about me?"

"I'll never tell."

When they walked in to the Wagon Wheel Steak House, Dallas asked the host if they could have a table or a booth out of the way where they could be alone.

"Sure, right this way." He guided them to a back room where they were all by themselves. "How is this?"

"This is just great," Dallas said as he helped Shay with her chair.

"Do you come here often?" Dallas asked.

"No, I've only been here once or twice. Why do you ask?"

"By the way the guy's looked at you when we came in, I thought you must have been here before."

"Oh, right, nobody even noticed. Would that make you jealous?"

"No, they can look if they want, but you're with me."

"I was hoping it would make you jealous."

They ordered and sat and sipped on their Cokes and talked of things that had happened since they last saw each other.

"What's been going on out at the ranch?" asked Shay.

"Oh, the same old thing that you do every day on a ranch."

"No, I mean, has anything unusual gone on?"

"No, what do you mean?"

"Well, I've been nosing around, and Sue, my best friend who works at Jippem Real Estate, is keeping her ears open. I just have a strange feeling that Mr. Jippem wanting to buy your ranch is a funny deal. He told me that you never know how much trouble you can have around a ranch. I just have the feeling that he might do something to persuade you to sell."

"Why do you think that?"

"The day I quit, he said something about how he was going to get that ranch, and you could never tell what might happen to encourage you to sell."

"You know, now that you mention it, remember when you and I were out riding and heard those gunshots?"

"Yes."

"Well, Hank and one of the guys went out the next day and looked around to see if they could find where somebody had dressed out a deer, but they didn't find anything, and I never gave it anymore thought. We did have a couple of cows come up missing, but that happens all the time, and we usually find it within a week or so in another part of the pasture."

"I just feel that there's something funny about this deal. They seem to want your ranch and no other. It's the land they're after because Jippem said they would probably tear the buildings down. Then there's the fact that they don't want to give you what the land is worth. Jippem seemed to know that your mortgage is due, and he thinks he can buy it for fifty cents on a dollar because you'll have to sell or the bank will foreclose."

About that time, their food came, and Dallas said, "Can I say Grace?"

"Please do." He reached across the table and took Shay's hands in both of his and bowed his head. Shay didn't bow her head or close her eyes. She was taking in the picture of the handsome man who sat across the table from her.

"Dear Lord," Dallas started, "thank you for letting me find Shay today. Be with her, guide and protect her, and help her to find another job. We thank you for this time we can spend together. May our conversation and actions be pleasing to you. Thank you for this food and bless it to our body's use. Amen." He squeezed her hands, and when he looked up, he noticed she had tears in her eyes.

"Why the tears, Shay? Did I say something wrong?" She didn't say anything for a few minutes but just sat there and held his hands and looked at him.

"You're such an unusual man. You're tough but tender. You're all man but have self control. You're handsome but not proud. You know what you want, but you think of others. You like women but treat them right. I would like to know what controls you, what makes you tick?"

"Why, thank you, I couldn't have said it much better myself."

"Dallas, can't you ever be serious?"

"I'm proud that you think I'm such a good guy. It makes me feel real great. I was none of those things you mentioned before I gave my life to Jesus Christ, but he changed my whole attitude and the way I treat people. Oh, I still goof up once in a while, but on the whole, I'm a better man than I used to be." About that time, the waitress came with their check and asked if she could get them anything else. That ended the conversation they were having.

They went to one of the nice parks not far from where Shay lived and spent the rest of the afternoon lying on a blanket and getting to know each other.

"When do you have to go back?" Shay asked.

"Tonight, I have some neighbors coming in the morning to help work some of the cattle, and I better be there for that. Besides, I better let you get on with finding a new job."

"Oh, that's not important. I thought I would take off a few days before I started that."

"Well, don't go too long. If you don't have a job, you have no money. If you have no money, you don't eat. If you don't eat, you get thin, and I don't want that. You're just right the way you are."

"You haven't seen me without clothes. I have to lose at least ten pounds before summer and swimsuit season gets here." He just looked at Shay with a gleam in his eye. "What?"

"I was just picturing you in a swimsuit."

"Pretty fat, right?"

"Not the girl I see."

"Let's just drop it. How did we get on this subject?"
"You were just telling me how good you looked in a swimsuit."
"Dallas, drop it."
He just smiled but said no more.

They stopped at the Dairy Queen and had a sandwich before he had to go back to the ranch, but he still couldn't pull himself away and get on the road.

Along about ten-thirty, Shay said, "I don't want to chase you out of here, but you have at least three hours to drive, and you have to get up in the morning to work, so I want you to get out of here."

"Well, thank you! When you came to my place, I wouldn't let you go. I made you stay overnight and now here you are throwing me out!"

"I'm not throwing you out. You wouldn't stay even if I asked."

"How do you know?"

"Okay, will you stay? You can sleep on the couch."

"No, what kind of guy do you think I am?"

"Get out," she said shaking her head.

"Shay, as long as you're not working or even looking for a job, why don't you come out to the ranch this weekend?"

"Are you asking me just because you don't think I have anything to eat, or do you really want me to come?" she said with a grin.

"If you don't come, I am coming after you."

"Okay, I'll be there."

"Come out Friday and make it a long one."

"We'll see."

Shay followed him to the door, and he reached to open it but stopped. He turned to her and put his arm around her pulling her close. "I think we've begun a lasting friendship, and I like it."

"Me too," she replied, and she tipped her head up for their first kiss that she never got. He closed the door behind him, and he was gone.

Shay stood there stunned! What just happened? He didn't kiss her! Most men would've been all over her by this time. They would've begged to stay overnight, and they wouldn't have wanted to sleep on the couch. Why was he so different? Was it her?

CHAPTER SEVEN

Shay turned on the television and watched the end of the *The O'Reilly Factor*, but she didn't know what he was talking about. She was thinking of the man who just walked out. Who was he? They had just spent most of the day together and talked of their childhood and growing up, but she still didn't know who he was. He had such inner peace. The next time they were together, she was going to question him more about this Jesus thing. She hadn't gone to church much as a kid, only on Easter and Christmas, and that was about it. It was the thing to do, but to go anymore than that was out of the question. Her father worked hard all week, and the weekend was meant for fun. They spent a lot of time at the lake and going to ball games and the like. Church was okay for the weak and women, but her dad said they didn't have time for it.

This was Monday. It was going to be a long time until Friday when she could see Dallas again.

She spent the next few days seeing if she could find out why Jippem wanted the Z bar 3 so badly, but she didn't have much luck. She talked to Sue, and the only information that she got from her was that Jippem and Barry had spent a lot of time together the last few days. Then she did some shopping for Western clothes. She could hardly go back out to the ranch and expect Martha to supply her with clothes like she had the last time. She got three pairs of jeans and some really nice shirts. A hat and some boots finished out her wardrobe.

Thursday morning, she awoke to a bright sunny day with very little wind, which was unusual for South Dakota. She could stand it no longer, and although Dallas told her to come out on Friday, she decided to go a day early. She already had her bags packed, so without eating anything, she went out to her car. Putting the top down, she started down the street to the interstate. Just before she pulled on to the four-lane, she filled up with gas and got a cup of coffee and a couple of donuts. The warm May breeze blowing in her blond hair was a wonderful feeling. She hoped that Dallas wouldn't be upset because she came a day early. If he was busy, she would just spend the day helping Martha.

Just before she got to the Missouri, she headed north, back into the West River country. It was a beautiful land except for the lack of rain, which had turned everything brown instead of the green it should be this time of the year. The tar road soon turned to gravel, and Shay slowed to match the road conditions.

At Tumble Weed, she pulled into the gas station/general store/whatever-else-you-needed to top off her gas tank and get another cup of coffee and maybe a snack or sandwich. Shay was leaning up against the back fender of her Mustang while the gas pump was grinding away, filling her tank.

"What are you doing out here again?' came a voice behind her. She turned to see a girl in her late teens dressed in cowboy attire, glaring at her from the other side of the car.

"Excuse me?" said Shay.

"Are you hard of hearing? I said what are you doing out here again?"

"Who wants to know?"

"I'm Gretchen, and I'm telling you to stay away from my man."

"And who would that be?"

"You know who you're chasing. This is the second time you've been out here trying to steal him from me. Well, I'm telling you, he's mine and you leave him alone."

"You still haven't told me who your man is."

"Dallas Ziglar," said Gretchen. There was fire in her eyes.

"I'm not here to steal anybody's man. Mr. Ziglar and I are doing some business together."

"Oh." She turned and walked over and got in a dirty old truck and drove off. So Dallas already had a girl, and he was just playing her for a sucker. Gretchen was kind of young, but maybe that's why he hadn't made a pass at her. She was just too old for his liking.

There was a small lunch counter at one end of the store where she got a hamburger and a Coke. This was a real hamburger—two slices of bread with the meat hanging out on all sides—chips and half dozen pickles, all for half the price you would pay in Rapid City. She sat at one of the checkered tableclothed tables and started in on her lunch. It was fun just watching the people come and go. Nobody seemed to be in a real hurry either in the general store or around the gas pumps, taking time to talk to each other. Most of the conversations either had to do with how dry it was or how low the cattle prices were. Every kind of vehicle you could imagine filled up with gas or diesel at one of the three pumps in front of the store, and it must have been some kind of unspoken rule that if you got fuel, you had to have a cup of coffee and a donut. Most of the patrons were men although there were a few women who stopped for some groceries. Shay finished the last of her sandwich, paid her check, and got another cup of coffee for the road. She pulled away from the pumps out on to the road and almost decided to turn back to the interstate and leave Dallas to this girl of his. But he did tell her to come out or he would come and get her. Was he serious or just playing with her feelings? Now that she was a day early, would he think she was chasing him?

Down the road another twenty miles, she came to the sign:

YOU ARE NOW ENTERING THE Z bar 3 RANCH

Another five miles, she turned in the main gate for the two-mile drive up to the headquarters. As she topped the last hill and the big house came into view, she had a sense of being home. Did she really belong here, or was this just wishful thinking? Stopping in front of the main entrance, she sat for just a minute, taking in the view of the house. It was just as she had remembered it, and she wasn't dreaming. It was more magnificent than the first time she was here.

She walked up the steps, across the porch, and knocked on the door. She waited. It seemed like an eternity before she heard footsteps approaching, and the door opened.

"Shay!" Martha threw her arms around her. "It's so good to see you. Dallas said you were coming, but I didn't expect you until tomorrow."

"I know. I hope it's not an imposition for me to be here a day early?"

"Oh, not at all. I'm glad you came early, and I know Dallas will be too. He and Hank took off early this morning. They're checking on some cattle down in the south pasture."

"Maybe later, I should ride down and see if I can find them," said Shay.

"Oh, you might get lost down there."

"I won't go that far from the house. If I don't find them, at least I'll get a nice ride out of the deal. It's such a nice day."

"Come in. Let me make you some lunch before you go."

"No, I stopped in Tumble Weed and had a hamburger."

"Aren't they some hamburgers? That Joe does a good job," said Martha.

"They sure are! That hamburger is a meal in itself."

"At least have a cup of coffee and talk to me a bit."

It was later, much later, that Shay said, "If I'm going to catch those guys out in the south pasture, I better get going."

Shay walked down to the corral that Midnight was in the last time and found her there. A ranch hand was doing some work around one of the barns, and she asked if he could get a saddle for Midnight.

"You mean you are going to try riding that mare?"

"Yes, I think she likes me."

"Okay, I'll throw a saddle on her, but I sure hate to see a lady get dumped."

After a couple of rounds around the corral, Shay hollered to the ranch hand to open the gate, and she trotted on down the lane toward the south. The cowboy stood there with his hat in his hand scratching his head. He couldn't believe that girl had ridden Midnight.

It was so beautiful riding along the Missouri, and she stopped on the high ridge where she and Dallas had stopped the first day she was out there. She forgot about what she was looking for as she got down off of Midnight and stood there looking out across the river. This country was beginning to grow on her.

Dallas and Hank were on their way back from checking on the cattle much farther to the south.

"I'm going to ride over and check along the river and see how the cows are doing there," said Dallas. "You might just as well go on back to the ranch. I heard Martha say this morning she wanted you to run her into town this evening."

"Oh, she can go by herself."

"What kind of a husband are you anyway? You're supposed to do what your wife wants. You go ahead. Don't worry about me. I'll fix a sandwich or something for supper."

"Okay," said Hank. "I'll see you in the morning." He rode off to the north and over the next hill on his way toward the homestead.

Dallas worked his way up along the river, checking different draws as he went. As he topped one of the rises, far to the north he spotted a lone rider coming in his direction. *Now who could that be?* he thought to himself. Whoever it was, they were in no hurry. They seemed to be out for just a leisurely ride. He pulled out his field glasses and trained them on the rider. He couldn't believe his eyes. It was Shay! Putting his horse into a gallop, it wasn't long before he covered the ground that separated them.

"Hey there, good-looking, what you are doing in these parts?" Dallas hollered as his horse trotted up to her. "Man, am I glad to see you!" He reached out and laid his gloved hand on her arm. "I was afraid you wouldn't come."

"That's why I came a day early, so you didn't have to worry about it."

"I'm glad you did."

Dallas climbed down off his horse, and then he helped Shay down.

"You really look good in those cowboy duds. I haven't seen anything that fancy around this ranch. You must have brought your own."

"I thought it was about time I got my own clothes. When I come here, you feed me, and you give me a beautiful room to stay in. The least I can do is bring my own clothes."

"Oh, I'll buy them too if you want me to," he said. "Look," he whispered as he put his arm around her shoulders and pointed off in the direction of the river, "see those two deer coming down to drink?"

"Yes, aren't they beautiful?"

"Look, there's a fawn behind them in the tall grass," he whispered to her. They stood and watched them for a long time while several more deer joined the others.

The sun was dropping fast behind them, and Shay said, "We'd better get going before it gets dark."

"Let's stay here and watch the moon come up over the river again. Last night, it was so pretty, but you weren't here to watch it with me. I can find my way back after dark, that's if you trust me enough to be with me after dark."

"Don't you have to be home for supper?" asked Shay.

"No, Hank and Martha went into town. I told them I'd find something to eat later."

"Oh good, it's so nice out here," she said. "Dallas?" He was watching another doe and fawn farther down the shore with his binoculars.

"What?"

She didn't answer.

"What?" he said lowering the field glasses and looking at her. She was staring off across the river. He looked in the direction that she was staring at. "What?"

"What's wrong with me?"

He looked at her in surprise. "I don't know. Is there something wrong with you?"

She turned toward him and asked, "Do you find me attractive?"

"Is this a trick question?"

"Dallas, I'm serious."

"Okay, I find you more than attractive. You're gorgeous. You're charming and lovely. You're sexy and magnificent. You're—"

"Okay, okay,"—she held her hand up for him to stop—"that's enough. Then what's wrong with me?"

"What do you mean?"

"Here we sit on the banks of a beautiful river, with the moon coming up, scattering diamonds across the water, and you haven't even tried to hold my hand or make a pass at me. The other night when you left my condo, you never even tried to kiss me. Most guys would have at least tried something."

"I'm not most guys, and besides, I don't dare."

"What do you mean you don't dare? Do you think I'll slap your face or something?"

"No, I don't trust myself. I'm a red-blooded American boy who has all the desires of a man. If you don't want to be taken in by the heat, you stay away from the fire. You are way too beautiful and sexy for me to take the chance. I've asked God to keep me pure and save myself for the woman I will someday marry. Don't you think I should do my part to help him?"

"You have got to be kidding! I've never heard a guy talk that way. Most of them have been after all they can get. That's why I hardly ever date. If I want a wrestling match, I'll watch WWF on television."

"You must be dating the wrong kind of guys."

"I didn't know there were guys like you."

"I couldn't do it on my own, but God helps me. I am just a powerless man."

"I don't understand. God helps you?"

"Yes, after I gave my heart and my life to him, he forgave me of my sins and set me on a new path. He helps me not to make those mistakes again, not do wrong, and keep my life clean. When you get married, do you want a guy that's been with every bimbo up and down the street?"

"No, I see what you mean."

"I don't want that either."

Shay grabbed both of Dallas's hands as they sat there in the grass. "Let's get this straight right off the bat. I want you to know right now that I've kept myself pure too even though I don't know much about this religion stuff."

Dallas took Shay into his arms and held her tight as he whispered, "Thank you for telling me that."

When he released her, she looked at him and said with a grin on her face, "That didn't bother you too much, did it?"

"No, I can handle that as long as I don't hold you too long."

"Does that mean we are courting now?"

"No, we're working on our friendship. Remember I told you that someday I wanted to marry my best friend and why work on a friendship with someone you would never marry?"

"That's amazing! I have never heard anything like this before."

"Did you start reading that Bible I gave you?"

"I read John and started Luke."

"That much already? That's great! Next time you come, I want you to write down some questions you have, and let's talk about it."

"You mean you're going to let me come back another time?"

"You better."

"I'll put some questions together. I do want to learn more about the Bible."

They sat for a long time just enjoying being together and watching the moon on the river far below them.

"Can I ask you another question?" asked Shay.

"Sure, I probably won't answer it but you can ask."

"Who's Gretchen?"

"How do you know about Gretchen?"

"My question first."

"Gretchen lives on the next ranch to the west. We went to school together. How do you know her?"

"Is she your girl?"

Dallas looked at Shay and smiled. "Hardly, I said we went to school together, but when I graduated from high school and went to college, she was in the fifth grade. Now how do you know her?"

"But seven years doesn't make that much difference. What do you think about her now? Do you love her?"

"Shay"—he looked her right in the eye—"if I loved her, do you think I would be out here with you right now?"

"Well," she said and paused for a long time. "I guess not."

"Trust me, dear, I have no feelings for Gretchen or any other woman."

"What did you call me?"

"I asked if you saw that deer?" he said with a grin on his face.

"God isn't getting much help from you, is he?" Shay asked.

"Now my question, how do you know Gretchen?"

"I stopped for gas in Tumble Weed. She came up and told me to stay away from her man. I asked her who she was, and she said her name was Gretchen."

"Gretchen said that?" He laughed. "What did you say?"

"I asked her who her man was, and she said Dallas Ziglar, then I said not to worry, Mr. Ziglar and I were doing some business together. All she said was 'Oh' and got in her truck and left. I felt sorry for her."

"Did you lie to her? Is that why you came out here, only to do some business? I thought you came because you liked me."

"Well, maybe a little white lie."

"For all have sinned and come short of the glory of God."

"What?"

"You just admitted that you are a sinner. Lying is a sin, and you need God to forgive you."

"That was only a white lie. That doesn't count," answered Shay. "You know if I keep coming back after a while, I might get to like you."

"Keep coming," he replied and squeezed her hand.

"Dallas, look at me." He turned toward her. "Do you belong to Gretchen?"

"No, Shay, I couldn't love her even if I tried. She just doesn't turn me on like . . ."

"Like?"

"Never mind."

"I'll have a talk with Gretchen," said Dallas.

"No, you won't. That would be mean. Let me handle it. She doesn't deserve to have her self-image wrecked."

He took Shay by the hand and helped her up and lifted her into the saddle. He wanted to take her into his arms and hold her, but he prayed, *Lord, help me here. I'm losing control.*

BANG! BANG! BANG! BANG!

"What was that!" shrieked Shay.

Off to the southwest, several gunshots rang out.

"That's gunshots!"

"Who's shooting, and what are they shooting at? It's dark!"

"I don't know, but it probably isn't good. Hank and I will have to check it out in the morning."

"You know the last time I was out here, there was a gunshot. Did you ever check that one out?"

"No, I kind of forgot about it. But we'll check this one out."

They didn't have to do much on the way home since the horses knew the way. They just sat and enjoyed the ride in the moonlight without even talking. Shay helped him put the saddles away and take care of the horses.

When they walked into the kitchen, there was a note on the table.

Guy's,

Supper is in the oven. I hope it's still warm. I turned down your bed, Shay. I'll see you at breakfast.

Martha

"What a sweet lady. How did you manage to get such a wonderful person?"

"Oh, I just attract all the sweet ones. Look at the one I have here."

They were still sitting in the great room talking when Hank and Martha got home, but the lights were turned down low, and they didn't even see Dallas and Shay sitting there.

"Don't tell me those kids already went to bed," said Hank as he got a glass of milk and a couple of cookies and sat down at the kitchen table.

"I think so," said Martha. "Shay's door is closed. She was probably pretty tired after driving all the way out here from Rapid City."

"Boy, she sure is a nice girl," said Hank. "If that Dallas don't latch onto her, I'm going to beat him over the head with a two by four."

"Yes, she is sweet, but if they do get married, she'll probably have to ask him. You know how easygoing he is. He may not ever get around to asking her."

Shay looked at Dallas and could hardly keep from laughing.

"Well, he better be good to her. He was kind of hard on her the first time she was out here. I don't know why she just didn't slap the tar out of him."

"Oh, he was just having fun. You know what a tease he is."

"Yes, and you baby him. You're so good to him he don't need a wife."

"Well, he is just like our own son."

"I'm going to tell him tomorrow," said Hank, "not to let Shay get away. A girl like that don't come around very often. I don't know of one that good-looking since you came."

"Oh, Hank, you old fox, let's go to bed."

"Don't say anything to Shay about getting married. This is only her second time out here. We don't want to scare her off."

"You know, I think the other day when he went into Rapid City after supplies, he might have gone to see her. He sure got home late. I don't know of any stores open that time of the night."

"Do you think so?"

"Yes, I do. He sure was in a good mood the next day, and it wasn't because he got a lot of sleep that night."

With that, they turned out the kitchen light and went down the hall hand in hand.

Dallas reached over and took Shay's hand. "See what you're doing? You got them ganging up on me."

"No, I just have them fooled, but I'm glad they like me. I just wish I could fool you that easy."

He slid over closer to her and took her in his arms. "Can we pray together?" he asked.

"Sure."

"Dear Lord, thank you for bringing Shay into my life. Help me to treat her in the way that she should be treated. May our relationship be honorable in your sight. Help her to realize how much you love her. Amen."

He held her for a long time, very close. When he released her, she was crying.

"What's wrong, dear?"

"Nobody has treated me or cared for me like you have. Hank and Martha too. I don't know what to say or how to act. What can I give in return?"

"Nobody is looking for anything from you. Just be yourself. That's who people like." He let her go and sat back with his hand on his forehead. "Man, I have to stop that! I'm losing control. I better go to bed." He stood up.

"Don't worry, Dallas, I won't let you. I respect you too much to let you get carried away," she replied with a serious look on her face. He knew she meant it.

"Are you going to sleep in your clothes, or did you bring some bags with you?"

"Maybe I should bring in a bag or two, but it's none of your business what I sleep in."

Dallas reached down and took Shay by the hand. "Come on, I'll go with you to get your bags, to protect you from all the wild animals."

"It's this big bad wolf that I am afraid of," she said and squeezed his hand and smiled up at him.

As they stopped in front of her bedroom door, he took both of her hands in his and said, "I would like to stay up all night talking to you, but you do strange things to me, and I am afraid I can't control myself much longer."

"I know what you mean. I told you I wouldn't let you get carried away, but the way I feel right now, I'm not sure how much help I would be."

"Good night, Shay." He patted her on the shoulder and walked down the hall to his bedroom as she stood there and watched him go.

"God, if you are there," she prayed, "thank you for Dallas and the way he treats me."

In minutes, they were both asleep together, but apart.

CHAPTER EIGHT

Dallas was sitting at the table having his first cup of morning coffee while Martha and Shay were busy getting breakfast ready.

Hank walked in the kitchen and said, "Sure smells good. What are we having?"

"It must be nice to sleep in like that," Dallas said. "No wonder we can't get anything done around this ranch, when the help can't get up in the morning."

"Well, I'm not as young as you. I can't stay up all night like you do chasing women."

"You better not," said Martha. "Besides, you wouldn't know what to do if you did catch one." Martha put the breakfast on the table while Shay filled everybody's coffee cup. They all held hands while the blessing was said. This was something special for Shay. She had never asked the blessing before, and she didn't know anybody that did. But it made sense—if God provided all this for them, it was only right you thank him for it.

They started eating, and Dallas said, "You know, Hank, when Shay and I were riding in after dark last night, we heard several gunshots."

"After dark you say? What made it so late? Did you have some trouble along the way?"

"No, everything was fine. We just got in a little late."

"Oh, I see." He had a smile on his face. "What do you think the shots were?"

"I don't know, but I think we better do some checking this morning."

"Good idea, I'll get some of the boys to help us."

"No, I'm going to do something I vowed I would never do, but I'm going down and see if I can get that old Piper Cub running. You can cover so much more ground with the cub than you can on horseback."

"But, Dallas," said Martha, "you haven't flown for several years. You're going to go out there and kill yourself."

"I know, but it's like riding a bicycle—once you learn how, you never forget it. It's time I put the memory of my folks' crash behind me and move on."

"I still don't think you should do it," said Martha.

"Yes, Mom, I know you don't, but I'll be okay."

"Are you sure you should do this?" asked Shay with fear in her eyes.

"I'll be okay. I wouldn't do it if it was dangerous."

"Yeah right," said Martha, "he's always doing dumb things."

"Hank, can't you control your wife?"

"Are you kidding? I don't even try anymore."

"Where are those walkie-talkies, Martha?"

"In the hall closet."

"Hank you take one, and I'll take the other one in the plane. If I spot anything, I'll let you know."

"I'm going with—" said Shay.

"No, you're not," answered Martha. "He can go and kill himself in that stupid airplane if he wants to, but you're not going up with him."

"No, I'm not going in the plane. I'll ride along with Hank."

"Oh, I should have known you're too smart to get in that dumb airplane."

"If Dallas would take me, I would go," said Shay. "I trust his judgment."

"Well, thank you, I'm not going to take any chances."

Hank and Dallas got in one of the ranch pickups, and Shay slid in the front seat between them, and they drove up to the hanger.

"I wonder if the battery is still up on that Cub. We may have to prop it."

"No," said Hank, "I charged it up a couple of weeks ago. I had an inkling it wouldn't be long, and you would be flying again."

"Hank, I think I'll just go to Florida for a month or two and let you and Martha run the place. Both of you know what I am going to do before I even do it. I don't know what I would do without you two!"

"I know it. We're just great people," answered Hank with a grin on his face.

"See what I have to put up with, Shay?"

"What are we going to do with Shay? We don't want her around here. Can she go with you to Florida?"

"Wait a minute," said Shay. "It's not up to you two to decide what I do. What makes you think I want to go to Florida, and if I did, why would I go with Dallas?"

By this time, they were at the hangar. They got the doors open and rolled the Cub out onto the apron.

"This bothering you?" asked Hank.

"No, it's time to get over it," answered Dallas. "It's been almost two years. Dallas walked all around the plane, giving it a thorough inspection as Shay watched with great interest. This wasn't some careless kid out taking a chance with a new toy, but a man who was careful and confident about what he wanted to do. She didn't know anything about airplanes or flying, but she could tell he was meticulous in his inspection.

After checking over the engine, Dallas climbed in. "Clear," he hollered and hit the starter. It turned over half a dozen times and roared to life. He tested the controls and taxied out on to the runway, testing the mags and others on the way. He paused for just a second and then opened the throttle, and the plane started to roll down the runway. A couple of hundred feet and the Cub lifted into the air and continued to climb. Hank and Shay stood there and watched as he banked to the left and leveled off. He came back around and came in for a landing. As the wheels touched the ground, he gave it full power again and was in the air.

"What is he doing?" asked Shay with a touch of fear in her voice. "Is he in trouble?"

"No, that's what they call a touch-and-go landing. He's just getting the feel of the airplane again. Dallas is a real good pilot, but he hasn't flown since his folks were killed. Once he gets it in his blood again, you won't be able to keep him on the ground. That airplane can do the work of a half dozen horses and riders."

Dallas came back around again and landed, taxiing up to the hangar. Without shutting off the engine, he hollered, "Come on, Shay, I'll give you a ride." There was a look of satisfaction written on his face. Shay ran out to the plane without hesitation and climbed in the backseat of the tandem-seat Piper.

"Find the seat belt okay?" Dallas hollered above the noise of the engine.

"Yes, I got it."

"Are you scared?"

"Nope."

"Good, here we go." And he waved at Hank.

As they taxied out to the runway, Hank got in the truck and headed back for the ranch.

Dallas gave the plane full power, and as Shay watched the ground fall away, she put her hand up on his shoulder and said, "Oh, this is wonderful! You can see forever from up here."

"Is this the first time you have been in a small plane?"

"Yes, I didn't realize how much fun it would be."

They circled back over the buildings as they watched Hank pull up and go in one of the barns. They made a complete circle and headed south into the wilderness country. As they went, they could see cattle scattered in different areas, trying to find something to eat in the parched, dry landscape.

"How far this way does the ranch go?" Shay asked.

"About six miles."

"How high are we?"

Dallas looked at the altimeter and said, "Four hundred feet." They flew to the south line and turned around and headed back for the ranch. All the time, Dallas was scanning the ground below him for something that didn't look right. All of a sudden, he said, "Over there, that's what I was afraid of!" He pointed off to the east.

"What?"

"See those cows over there? They're lying on their side." He banked in that direction.

"So?"

"Cows don't lie on their side unless they are sick or dead." He made a low pass over where the cattle were and then climbed back up to about five hundred feet. He picked up the walkie-talkie and said, "Hank, this is Dallas. Do you read me? Over."

"Yeah, Dallas, I read you loud and clear, over."

"I'm over section 28, and I don't like what I see. Do you want to take a look? Over."

"Yes, I see where you are circling. I'll head in that direction, over."

"I'm going to fly on up to the homestead to see if there's anything else. I should be back before you get here in case you can't find them. Over"

"Okay, over and out."

They flew on north to the homestead where they turned around and headed back south. By the time they got back to the spot, Hank was already there. They watched as he rolled some of the cattle over and surveyed the situation.

"Dallas, Hank here, there are two horse tracks that came in from the west road and went back the same way. These cattle have been shot. Do you want me to follow them? Over."

"No, that's a long way over there. We'll take the pickup around the road and see what we can find. You may as well go back home. I'm going to fly up to the north line and see what's going on up there. Over."

"Okay, I'll see you at lunch. Over and out."

Shay and Dallas turned and flew up along the river to the north line and then went west about a mile and flew back to the ranch. There was no breeze at all, so it didn't make any difference which way they landed, so Dallas came straight in from the northwest and touched the wheels onto the tar in a smooth landing.

When they were rolling the plane back into the hangar, Shay said, "That was fun for you, wasn't it?"

"Yes, I had kind of forgotten how much fun flying was. You can sure check the cattle in a hurry from the air. We've wasted a lot of time just because I was too stubborn to fly again."

"You weren't stubborn. Some of these things just take time."

He looked at her and said, "You're good for me, Shay." He took her hand. "We better get with it. We don't want Martha to have to wait lunch for us." They started on down the road in the direction of the house.

As they sat down at the table, Dallas said, "What do you make of those dead cattle? What were there, eight or ten?"

"Twelve."

"I better call the sheriff.'

"Already did," said Hank, "said he'll be out in a couple of hours. He was just west of Tumble Weed when I go hold of him."

"We can meet him at the main gate and go on south from there."

After they had said Grace and started eating, Shay said, "That was sure a lot of fun flying over the countryside."

Martha dropped her fork and looked at Shay, "He didn't talk you in to going up in that crate, did he?"

"No, he just asked if I wanted to, and I accepted."

"Shay, I thought you were smarter than that." She shook her head.

"Tomorrow I'm going to give you a ride, Martha," said Dallas with a big grin on his face.

"Not me, I am ready to die, but I don't want to die tomorrow." And everybody laughed.

"Dallas, will you give me a hand on the clutch of that John Deere that I've been working on for the last few days?" asked Hank. "I just can't get it lined up by myself."

"Sure, let's do it."

"Good," said Martha, "Shay can help me make a couple of pies for supper."

It didn't take them too long to get the clutch back in place and bolted down, and Dallas said to Hank, "We'd better get going. The sheriff should be coming past the main gate before too long."

"Let me go in the house and see if Shay wants to ride along," said Dallas

As he walked into the kitchen where Martha and Shay were just finishing up their pies, Dallas asked, "You coming, Shay?"

"May I?"

"Sure."

"May I come too," asked Hank who was right behind him with a grin on his face.

"I guess if you really want to."

They weren't at the gate but a few minutes when they saw the sheriff coming down the road in his pickup truck, the dust boiling up behind him.

He said, "I'll follow you guys to where you think the riders came out." They drove on south about six miles and then stopped alongside of the road, being careful to not drive on any of the other tracks. They all got out of their vehicles and started looking around.

"Here, Jim, is where it looks like they came out. See, there were two riders, and right here is where they loaded the horses into a trailer."

"Yeah, they sure did," said the sheriff as he looked at where the horse tracks got up into the trailer. He checked the tire tracks of the truck and trailer.

"My guess is it's an older trailer. The trailer tires don't have much tread left. The truck too, a four-wheel drive with a bald tire on the back passenger's side."

"How do you know it's a four-wheel drive?" asked Shay.

"Because of the mud and snow tires on the front. You wouldn't put them on the front of a two-wheel drive truck." One of the deputies took plaster casts of a couple of the tire tracks and a lot of pictures.

"One of the guys smoked. Here's a cigarette butt, no filter. Get a couple of pictures of these boot tracks too, will you, Scott?"

"Well, Dallas," said Jim, "I think that's about all we can find here. I'm going to see if I can follow these tire tracks and see which way they turn when they hit the main road. If they turn north, I'll go into Tumble Weed and check trucks and tires at the bar."

"Anything you want us to do?" asked Dallas.

"Not for right now. Keep your eyes and ears open, and it wouldn't hurt to do a little flying and keep an eye on the whole ranch as much as you can. I'll be in touch with you if I find anything."

The sheriff and his deputy went on south, and after looking around a little more, Dallas said, "We might just as well go back to the ranch."

"Who in the world would shoot a bunch of cattle and why?" asked Hank.

"That's easy," said Shay. "Jippem wants to buy the ranch. He knows that times are hard right now with the cattle price down and no rain, and the pastures are drying up. Anything that goes wrong, or he can help go wrong, makes you more inclined to sell."

"Oh, I don't think he wants to buy so bad he would do anything like that," said Dallas.

"No, he wouldn't," answered Shay, "but he has people or knows people that would do it for a price."

"Do you really think so?"

"I know so. I've seen him use some pretty shady tactics in the past."

"Does he really want my ranch that bad?"

"Yes, he does. I don't know why just yet, but I aim to find out," said Shay.

"No, Shay, you stay out of this. I don't want you getting hurt."

Shay looked at Hank and said, "Do you remember me being hired on at the Z bar 3?"

"No, can't say that I do."

"Well, if I'm not a ranch hand, I don't have to take orders from Mr. Ziglar either, do I?"

"No, probably not, but he is giving you good advise."

Dallas reached over and laid his hand on Shay's knee. "I know you aren't going to do what I tell you to, but please be careful." He didn't move his hand even after she told him she would be careful.

When they walked in the house, Martha was sitting in the great room watching the news on the big screen TV. She grabbed the arms of the overstuffed chair to help herself up. "I'll bet you guys are hungry. I didn't know if you were going to make it for supper or not."

"We sure are," said Dallas. "How about the lady, she's not a ranch hand you know." He grinned at her.

"No, she's a guest, so we have to treat her better."

"There," said Shay, putting her nose in the air. "I guess she told you."

After they finished their ice cream and strawberry shortcake Martha had for dessert, Hank said, "You guys can sit up all night and talk if you want to, but I have to get some sleep. I'm working class you know."

"Can I talk to you a minute, Shay?" Dallas motioned toward the great room. They went in and sat on one of the couches, and Shay looked at Dallas with a puzzled look in her eye.

"What do you want to talk to me about?"

"I don't know. Do I have to have something special? I just wanted to talk to you."

"You sly old fox, you."

They sat up and talked far longer than they should have. It was going to be hard to get up in the morning.

CHAPTER NINE

Shay awoke with the sun coming through the curtains, shining in her eyes. What time was it? Where was she anyway? As the fog cleared from her head, she realized she was at the ranch, and it must be late. Let's see, she came to the ranch on Thursday, Friday, and Saturday. This must be Sunday. She looked at her watch and realized it was already seven thirty. She splashed some water on her face, ran a comb through her golden hair, and put on just a touch of makeup before she left the room. As she opened her door and stepped out onto the balcony, she thought, *My, it's quiet. Everybody must be gone or still sleeping.*

Down the long spiral stairway to the main floor and into the kitchen, she tiptoed. Where was everyone? There sat Dallas at the kitchen table, reading his Bible with a cup of coffee in one hand.

He looked up as she entered. "Good morning, did you sleep well?"

"Sure did, nothing like sleeping all day. Where is everybody?"

"This is Sunday. It's pretty relaxed around here on Sundays."

"I thought every day was the same on a ranch," replied Shay.

"No, we try and have our work pretty well done up, so there isn't even much for chores to do. Sunday is supposed to be the day of rest, and we try to keep it that way."

"So what do you do all day?"

"Well, we go to church and—"

"Go to church, are you going to church?"

"Yes, and you're coming too."

"Me? I don't know. I don't know much about church."

"What do you need to know, you just go and listen and then you come home."

"But I haven't been to church in years."

"Shame on you."

"What do I wear?"

"What you have on is fine. A lot of the women wear jeans or slacks or something. You're in West River country, you know. The Lord looks on your heart, not on what you're wearing."

"But shouldn't you dress up? When I did go to church, mostly Christmas and Easter, everybody tried to outdress the next one, especially the women."

"A dress would be nice, but if you don't have one, jeans are just fine."

"What will Martha wear?"

"I guess she would wear a dress. She's a real classy woman, but if you wear jeans, I'll bet she does too."

"Oh, Dallas, I should have gone home yesterday."

"No, you shouldn't. I want you to go with us to church."

"Okay, but will you help me to know how to act?"

"Don't you worry, you'll do just fine."

After breakfast was over and the dishes were done, Martha said, "I guess I better get ready for church. We should leave here in forty-five minutes or so."

"Are you wearing a dress?" Shay asked.

"I don't know. What are you going to wear?"

"Well, I brought a dress, but I want to wear what the other women wear."

"Okay," she said, "if you wear a dress, so will I. Hank really prefers me in a dress on Sunday."

To be honest about it, Shay brought three dresses along, and she had a hard time deciding which one she should wear. Should she wear the more formal one? No, this is cowboy country and she was sure that would be to fancy. Finally she settled on a black shirtwaist dress with a full skirt. She put on a little more makeup and some simple earrings, ran a brush through her hair one more time, and decided that would have to do.

Shay stepped out of her room just as Dallas was coming down the hall.

"Wow," he said, "you get prettier every day."

"Why, thank you, you look pretty sharp yourself."

He was wearing black slacks and shirt, open at the neck, and a tan Western-cut jacket.

As they came down the stairs together, Martha came out of the kitchen, "Now there's a fine-looking couple. Hold it right there. Let me get a picture of you two."

They stopped on the bottom step with Shay on the floor in front of Dallas. He put his hands on her shoulders, and Martha took several shots.

"Now change places with Dallas in front. You will be more the same height."

About the time Martha was through, Hank came in and looked at what was happening.

"Just one more," Hank said, "give him a big kiss!"

"Are you kidding? I'm pretty fussy about who I kiss."

"Oh, come on, Shay," said Dallas, "he's the ranch foreman you know. You should do what he says."

"I don't work here, remember?"

About that time, a horn sounded and Hank said, "Sounds like we're ready to roll."

Shay looked at Dallas with a questioning look but said nothing. When they stepped out on the porch, she saw a big van waiting in the driveway loaded with people.

"Do they come and get you for church?" she asked.

"No," said Dallas, "that's the ranch van. We use it when a lot of us are going some place. No use driving several vehicles, not with the gas prices these days."

Shay was surprised. The van was almost full. They had to crowd in wherever they could. It was real cozy. Several of the guys she recognized as ranch hands and some she had never seen before.

Before Dallas got in, he said, "Guys, some of you haven't met Shay. This is Shay, an old family friend. Really, she isn't that old. Shay, these guys are supposed to work here. Some of them do. Joe is driving, and Kip is in the front with him. In the back is Rusty, Sam, and Fred, and here are Pedro, Bandit, and Swede and of course Hank and Martha. Okay, let's roll." He climbed in and shut the door.

"Where are we going?" Shay asked as Dallas put his arm up on the back of the seat to make more room.

"There's a church in Tumble Weed. We go there."

"Yes, I saw a church there when I was getting gas the other day."

"It's not a very big church, mostly ranchers from around the area. I think you'll like it."

"Hey, Shay," said Joe as he looked back over his shoulder from the driver's seat. "Are you going to walk in to church with me? I'd like to show some of those guys I can get the good-looking girls."

"Sure, why not?"

"Wait a minute. I thought you were going with me?" chimed in Dallas.

"You were taking me for granted. You never asked me. Joe did." Everybody laughed.

When they got to the church, the parking lot was almost full of pickup trucks and only one or two cars. Joe got out of the van, walked around, opened the side door, and helped Shay out. He put out his arm, and she took it, and they walked into the church with Dallas following behind. One of the first people they met as they walked in was Gretchen.

Shay dropped Joe's arm and put out her hand, "Good morning, Gretchen. Good to see you again."

"Mornin', Shay," Gretchen stammered.

"Hi, Gretch, how's your grandpa? I heard he's been sick," said Dallas.

"He's feelin' better."

"Right this way, Shay." He nodded toward a back pew. Joe had already taken a pew with some of the other ranch hands.

As they sat down, Shay leaned over and whispered to Dallas, "Poor Gretchen is really confused now. She doesn't know if I am chasing you or Joe."

"No, and the sad part of it is Joe kind of likes her."

"I feel sorry for her. I'm going to be a friend to her."

Soon the service started with some real lively music. They had a band with guitars, violins, drums, a bass, and a banjo. People were singing, clapping their hands, and really enjoying themselves. This was unlike any church Shay had ever been to. Before long, she caught herself tapping her foot and slapping her knee. She didn't know any of the words, but they showed them on the front wall, so at times, she even tried to sing along. After several songs, the pastor got up and said a prayer, which was more like he was just talking to somebody in the room. In fact, Shay did open her eyes once, just to see who he was talking to. When he got done, he said, "This morning we have a good quartet with us. They are not the Sons of the Pioneers. They are the Pioneers themselves. Please welcome the newly formed group, our own Pioneers." Everyone clapped as they looked around the room.

Joe, Kip, Pedro, and Dallas walked to the front, and Rusty sat down at the piano and started to play. Shay couldn't believe her ears. This was the same cowboy who saddled the horse for her a couple of days ago. He was really good and the guys started to sing "I'll Fly Away" in perfect harmony. When they finished, the congregation were on their feet, clapping and hollering for more. Rusty started to play, and the Pioneers sang two more songs. When the people begged for more, Dallas held up his hand. "That's all for now, folks. We have to give Pastor Wade time for his sermon." The men left the platform.

"Wow, you guys are really good!" said Shay as Dallas came back and sat down. "I see now why people like to come to church."

Pastor Wade said while he was still clapping, "Wasn't that just great, folks? We are planning an all-music night in a couple of weeks where we'll hear more of these guys, as well as our band, along with more of the great talent we have in this church."

Pastor Wade preached for about half an hour, most of which Shay didn't understand. She would have to ask Dallas later what some of the things he said meant. All in all, it was an enjoyable time, and she was sure that she would like to come back again. After the service, Dallas said, "I have to go and talk to one of the men before he gets away. I'll be back in a minute." He made his way to the other side of the church, shaking hands with several people as he went.

Shay was standing there by herself when one of the young ladies came up and introduced herself, "I'm Mary Walker. I haven't seen you here before."

"No, this is my first time. I am visiting Hank and Martha O'Dell and Dallas Ziglar. I'm also friends with Gretchen Olson." Out of the corner of her eye, she saw Gretchen turn, look her way, and then come in her direction.

"Hi, Shay, it is good to see you here this morning."

"Oh, Gretchen, it's good to see you again."

"Are you coming to the basket social week after next?" asked Gretchen.

"I don't know. I hadn't heard anything about it. I'm not sure I know what a basket social is."

"Oh, you city gals have to learn how to have fun. All of the girls make up a lunch basket, and the men bid on the one they want to have lunch with. All of the money goes to the new church fellowship center we're going to build."

"Well, I guess I would be interested if you'll help me with what I should put in my basket."

"Sure, I'll do that," Gretchen promised.

"I'll tell you what. Why don't you come into Rapid City the day of the social, and you and I will do some shopping for some new clothes to wear to the social?"

"Oh, that sounds like so much fun. Would you take the time to do that with me?" asked Gretchen.

"Yes, it's a date. I'll be in touch."

"Good, I have to run. Grandfather is waiting for me."

As she was hurrying away, Dallas came back to where Shay was standing.

"Hi, Mr. Z.," Gretchen exclaimed with a big smile on her face.

"Wow, what's she so happy about?" he asked Shay.

"I told you I would handle it."

"I don't know what you said or did, but it looks like it worked."

"Gretchen said her grandfather was waiting for her. Don't her folks come?"

"Her dad was here, but her mother died when Gretchen was seven or eight from breast cancer. Her dad and grandfather have done the best they can to raise her, but she really needs a woman to help her buy some nicer clothes and help her fix her hair. She really is a pretty girl if she just had a little style."

On the way home in the van, Shay said, "You guys really did a good job this morning. When are you going to cut a CD?"

"As soon as we get a sponsor," said Kip. "Pepsi is thinking about it." Everybody laughed.

"Who taught you how to play the piano like that, Rusty?" Shay asked.

"Oh, I picked it up last week from watching TV."

"Can't any of you guys be serious? You are really good."

"That's for sure," added Hank.

After eating another good meal that Martha had put in the oven before leaving for church, Hank slid his chair back and stretched and said, "I think I will take a nap. This is the day of rest, you know. You coming with me, Martha?"

"No, I am going to finish my book I started a couple of weeks ago."

"What are you reading?" asked Shay.

"Oh, just a silly novel. *Fly North* is the name of it. It's about this young guy who flew fisherman into the lakes in northern Minnesota, and the girl he rescued from a plane crash. It's really pretty good."

"I like to read," said Shay. "Maybe you'll let me borrow it when you're finished."

"Sure."

"Do you want to go for a walk, Shay, or are you going to take a nap too?"

"No, let's go for a walk up to the bench that overlooks the river."

Dallas grabbed a blanket off one of the couches in the great room as they went out the front door.

"What's the blanket for?" Shay asked.

"I don't want you to get your dress dirty. There's another place up to the north that I'd like to show you."

It was only about half a mile up to the spot that Dallas had in mind. "This is the highest point on the ranch, and you can see most of it from here. See that butte over there in the distance? That's almost on the south line. The road over there about three miles is the west line. The river is the east line, and to the north, there is no real marker, but it is up there about three miles. On a clear day, you can see the water tower in Tumble Weed."

"The more I see of this country, the more I love it," said Shay.

Dallas spread the blanket on the ground, and they sat down to enjoy the view.

"What did you think of church this morning?" Dallas asked.

"It wasn't anything like I thought church would be. I always thought church was boring. You really have good music and everybody took part. You guys were just great. I didn't realize you had such a nice bass voice. Do you guys sing a lot?"

"No, we just started singing together a couple of weeks ago. That was the first time we sang in church."

"How did you get started?"

"There's an old piano down in the bunkhouse, and one evening, I happened to stop down there, and Rusty was playing it. It was a song I knew, so I walked over by him and started singing. It wasn't long Kip and Pedro joined in. We sang a couple of songs, and when Joe came in, he started singing even before he got to where the rest of us were. After that, we got together a couple times a week. It's been a lot of fun."

"I didn't understand much of what the pastor said, but I suppose it will take a little while."

"Yes, the more you go, the more you'll understand,"

They spent most of the afternoon sitting and talking, and sometimes, they just lay and watched the clouds float by.

"Shay, what are you going to be when you grow up?" Dallas asked.

She didn't answer for a long time but finally said, "I always dreamed of having my own real estate office. That's the only reason I went to work for Jippem—to get some experience."

"Didn't you say your father was in real estate?"

"Yes, and I could go into one of his offices, but I kind of want to make it on my own before I do that. I don't want to just be the boss's daughter."

"So you want to be a businesswoman?"

"Well, for now at least."

"Do you ever plan on getting married and having some kids?"

"This isn't a marriage proposal, is it?"

"No, just trying to find out your plans and desires."

"I know it. I was just teasing you. Sure, I want to get married and have a family, but it has to be with the right man. Too many of my friends have gotten married, and two years later, they are in divorce court. That isn't the way I want to do it. When I get married, I want it to last a minimum of seventy-five years. What about you?" she asked.

"I thought I would live and die on this ranch with a beautiful wife, a couple of kids, and one of them would take over the ranch someday just like I thought I would. But the way things are looking right now, that may not happen."

"Haven't you ever thought of doing anything else?"

"No, not really, this has always been the thing to do. When I went to college, I did look at other opportunities, but I couldn't forget about the ranch."

"What about girls? You must have dated a lot of them."

"Oh, I've been out with a few, mostly in groups. My mother told me when I was just a teen, 'Never marry a girl you think you can live with. Marry the one you know you can't live without,' and I haven't found that girl yet."

"Are you looking?"

"I'm keeping my eyes open. What about you?"

"I was pretty serious about a boy back home in high school, and then I found out he was bragging around school how good I was in bed. I had never been to bed with him. That made me so mad I told him to get lost, and I haven't found a guy I can trust since. What's wrong with guys? They think all a girl is good for is to go to bed with. That's one thing I would never do until I was married. If I am good enough to go to bed with, I am good enough to wait for. I'm still mad." Dallas could see the fire in her eyes.

Dallas didn't say anything.

Finally Shay said, "I'm sorry. I shouldn't take it out on you. You've treated me like a gentleman should."

Dallas rolled over on the blanket and put his arm around Shay. "Have you looked at yourself in the mirror lately?"

"No, not really."

"Maybe you should. You would know why guys would like to take you to bed. You are awfully sexy."

"Oh, I am not."

"Is it okay if I think so?"

"Sure, I'd like that. I know I can trust you."

After that, they lightened things up a bit. They didn't want to get in trouble.

"Do we have to get back? Will Martha be waiting supper for us?"

"No, Sunday night is a help-yourself thing."

They stayed and talked for a while longer. It was just good being together.

CHAPTER TEN

Shay had gone back to Rapid City, and that was good and bad. Good because Dallas didn't get anything done when she was here. He wanted to spend all his time with her. Bad because when she wasn't here, he missed her so badly he didn't get much done either. He had never felt this way about anyone before, but she had captured his heart in the short time he had known her. There had been other women who came to the ranch before, looking for horses, some really good-looking ones too. But none of them had passed the high standards he had for a wife, and then there were always his mother and Martha who gave him advice whether he wanted it or not.

There was one girl who came to the ranch shortly after his parents were killed. He had spent quite a bit of time with her and finally sold her a horse. She was nice, pretty, and fun to be around. For some reason, Martha didn't like her and made no bones about letting Dallas know it. In spite of Martha's opposition, Dallas dated her a time or two. It was hard to admit it to Martha, but the more he saw of her, the less he liked her. She came from a family who had a lot of money, and she thought everybody should cater to her because of it. She was proud, selfish, and self-centered, and by the time it was all said and done, Dallas wished he had never sold her a horse. The only thing good about the whole thing was that the horse dumped her a couple of times, and he got to watch. She wasn't as good a rider as she thought she was. She wasn't hurt, but her pride was sure injured. He finally ended up buying the horse back, but it was worth it, just to get rid of her. The only thing Martha ever said was, "Check with me before you get serious about a girl again." And she grinned.

Then Shay came along, and Martha falls head-over-heels in love with her. What was a guy to do? Martha had nothing but good to say about her.

"But, Martha, Shay isn't a Christian! That's the number one thing on my list for a wife."

"Yes, I know, but Shay is a smart girl. Just as soon as she learns about Christ and what the advantages of being a Christian are, she'll accept him."

"How do you know that? You've only known her a short time. You don't know anything about her."

"I know genuine when I see it."

That was a conversation he and Martha had after the first time she was at the ranch, and the more Dallas got to know Shay, the more he was finding out Martha was right. They had spent a long time talking and getting to know each other in the few times they had been together. Shay had grown up in Houston, Texas, where her father was a real estate developer. Her mother and father were good people with high moral standards but didn't feel religion was important. She had gone to Minnesota to go to college because she liked the school, and then she came to Rapid City to her friend's hometown to work for a while.

Dallas had tried to talk Shay into staying, but she said she had some things she just had to do. Dallas had a feeling that it had to do with some of the things that were happening on the ranch. He told her not to get involved, but he was sure she wasn't listening to him.

Dallas decided to go out and fix the main gate. Somebody had run into one of them and broke a hinge. He took the repair and fencing truck with all the tools and portable welder. He had the gate jacked into place and the hinge pulled back into place and was already to start welding when he saw a car come over the hill about half mile to the north.

Now who could that be? he said to himself as he stood and watched them approach. *Another salesman. People around here can't afford to drive new Cadillacs.* They pulled up alongside of his pickup and rolled down the window.

"You don't know where I can find Mr. Ziglar?"

"You're looking at him."

The driver got out of the car and walked over to where he was working.

"Better leave that cigar in the car," he said to the hundred pounds overweight guy who was still struggling to pry himself out of the car.

"That's okay," he said. "I'll be careful."

Dallas took a ballpoint pen out of his shirt pocket and started writing the license number down on his hand.

"What are you doing?" asked the driver.

"Writing down your license number so I know who to tell the sheriff who started the prairie fire."

"Slick, put that damn stogie in the car. Sorry, Mr. Ziglar, Slick isn't too smart sometimes."

"Mr. Ziglar, I'm Barry Killmee, and I think I might have a deal that would be really good for you. I know that ranching is mighty rough right now, with no rain and the cattle price's like they are, but you got a real good piece of land here. I think I could sell it for you, and you could live on easy street. I got a client out of California who has flown over this piece several times and has really fallen in love with it. Now he has the cash—cash, I tell you—to take it off your hands. I can make the deal and even slip some under the table. You wouldn't have to pay taxes on all of it that way."

"Are you from Jippem Real Estate?" Dallas asked.

"No, not really, I've done some work for him, but I'm on my own. These big ones I like to handle myself. I like to see everybody gets a fair deal."

"What makes you think you can put a deal together if the three or four people Jippem sent out before couldn't get the job done?"

"Well, those two guys were kind of amateurs. They really don't know how to handle this big stuff. And that woman, she had the idea all she had to do is come out here and flash a leg or two, and she would have you eating out of her hand. She wasn't as classy a dame as she thought she was. I hear tell old man Jippem fired her. You just can't send a floozy like her to do a man's job. So what kind of price do I put down on this contract?" Barry asked.

"Fifty million."

"Okay," he laughed. "Really, what should I put down?"

"I told you, fifty million."

"You know I can't sell it for that."

"I don't want to sell it."

"But what are you going to do when your mortgage on this godforsaken ranch comes due? I'm just trying to help you out."

"I guess you don't have to worry about my mortgage, do you? If I do decide to sell, I'm going to get hold of that nice lady and see that she gets the commission."

"Oh, so that's what you want. Well, I can get you top dollar and bring you all the women you can handle, ones who know how to please a man, not that hussy who was out here before."

Dallas reached out and grabbed Barry by the necktie, dragging him over to the car. "Get off my land and don't you ever come back."

About that time, the fat boy came around the front of the car, hollering, "Get your hands off Barry." Dallas let go of Barry's tie and, with one powerful blow, hit Tubby flat in the nose and, as he was going down, dropkicked him in the groin. He doubled over in wrenching pain. Dallas walked over to the truck and pulled out a lasso. He slipped it over the guy's head and around his neck. The other end he fastened around the trailer ball on the bumper of the truck.

"What are you doing!" screamed Barry.

"I'm going to drag him off of my ranch. It's only about six miles."

"No, no, you can't do that."

"Are you going to stop me?"

"No, no, Mr. Ziglar, just let me get him in the car, and we'll leave and never come back. Please, please don't kill him."

Dallas took off his hat, scratched his head, and stood there thinking awhile. "Okay, get him out of here." He took the loop from around the guy's neck. Barry went over and took his partner by the arm and helped him up. Tubby managed to get to the car all the while holding his injured parts.

"We're sorry, Mr. Ziglar."

Dallas just stood there and watched, doing his best to keep from laughing. Barry turned his car around and headed back north. As he did, he hollered back at Dallas, "You blankity, blank, bully, we'll get even with you. When we get done, there won't be anything left of this ranch to sell." He hit the gas and threw dirt and rocks all over the place as he roared on down the road.

Dallas finished what he was working on and went back to the ranch, put the fix-it truck in the shed, and worked in the shop until supper. He poured himself a cup of coffee and sat down to visit with Martha while she finished getting the meal ready. It wasn't long before Hank came in, washed up, and joined Dallas at the table.

"Funny thing happened in town today. I stopped at Sandy's Bar and Grill for a hamburger, and while I was sitting there, I couldn't help but overhear two guys up at the bar. They looked like salesmen. The one guy said they had been southeast of town, looking for a place to hunt pheasants, when they came across these four cowboys who ordered them off their land. He said, they were sorry, but they didn't know they were on private property. Well anyway, he said the four of them got out of their pickup, pulled them out of the car, and started beating them up. They lassoed one guy and were going to drag him down the road behind their truck. He said the cowboys were just crazy and would have killed them if they hadn't got in the car and took off. They said the cowboy just stood there in the middle of the road and laughed at them. I heard them say they were going to round up a bunch of guys and come back and clean house. That doesn't sound like something our guys would do, but we are the only ranch southeast of town. What do you think?"

"You're telling me they said there were four cowboys?"

"Yes, that's what they said."

"These two fellows were driving a white Cadillac?"

"Yes."

"One big fat guy smoking a cigar and one smaller guy with a white shirt and tie?"

"Yeah, how did you know?"

"Do I look like four guys?"

"You didn't teach a couple of guys a lesson, did you?" asked Hank.

"I might have."

"Why?"

"They said some terrible things about Shay."

Dallas went ahead and told Hank and Martha the whole story.

"Man, they really had you upset. I don't think I've ever seen you that mad about anything."

"They can say anything they want about me or you, but when they started talking about Shay in a dirty way, I just lost my cool."

"Were you really going to drag that guy down the road?"

"No, but he thought I was."

"You know," said Hank, "with what's been going on around here, I think we better do more flying and keep our eye on things. Maybe all of the guys should start carrying radios so we can all keep in touch with each other."

"Good idea, also I think I'll get a hold of Sheriff Jim and let him know what's been going on. I talked to him the other day, and he still doesn't have any leads on who shot those cattle. "Another thing," said Dallas, "I have a suspicion that Shay is nosing around Jippem's office, and I'm afraid she might get hurt. I asked her about it the other day, and all she said was,

'Don't worry. I can take care of myself.' Jippem is determined to buy this ranch, and Shay thinks she's going to find out why. She believes there's something fishy going on, and I guess I am starting to think that way too. I guess if we were smart, we would be keeping a better watch on things around here. I've been spending most of my time trying to find a way to pay off the mortgage on that twenty thousand acres Dad bought. That's what put this whole thing in trouble in the first place. I've been praying a lot about it, but I just don't feel right about selling. That verse over in Proverbs keeps coming back to me, 'Trust in the Lord with all thine heart; and lean not upon thine own understanding. In all thy ways acknowledge him, and he shall direct thy paths.' It's the waiting that's hard, but I am not going to sell until the Lord tells me to."

"Good boy," said Martha, "I've been praying too that you would wait for the Lord's leading."

CHAPTER ELEVEN

As Shay drove out through the main gate of the Z bar 3, she was more determined than ever to find out what was going on. She was sure that Jippem was up to no good. There were plenty of ranches up for sale that he could buy. All he had to do was look in the Green Sheet. There were land auctions every week. Why was he so interested in this ranch?

When she came through Tumble Weed, she thought she saw Gretchen's truck parked at the general store, so she pulled in. She needed a Coke, anyway. She walked in and saw Gretchen at the other end, picking up some bread. Walking up to her, she said, "Hi, Gretchen, I thought that was your truck out there. How are you today?"

"Fine, what are you doing in town?"

"I'm on my way back to Rapid City. You're still planning on coming to Rapid shopping, aren't you?"

"Sure, Dad said it would be all right."

"Why don't you come the night before and stay overnight with me? That way we can get an early start. We can have most of the day to shop."

"Do you really want me to do that?"

"Yes, that would be fun! Maybe we could go to a movie or something that night."

"Okay," she said, "that would be great."

They were about to walk out of the store when a white Cadillac went roaring through town.

"Look at that crazy guy," said Gretchen. "You'd think he'd slow down and not raise so much dust." Shay stared after the car. If she wasn't mistaken, that was Barry Killmee's Cadillac. *What in the world is he doing out here? I'll bet he is on his way to the Z bar 3.*

Later that day, when Shay walked into her condo, she noticed the light on the answering machine was flashing. She set down the things she was carrying and pushed the replay button.

"Where are you? We need to talk. Don't call me." That was Sue's voice. Next message, "We need to talk. Don't call me." Why shouldn't I call her? Third message, "Don't call." That was the last one. Sue sounded desperate, but why didn't she want Shay to call her? Shay was unpacking her suitcase when the phone rang.

"Hello."

"Meet me at Jill's Place!" *Click.*

It was Sue. Why couldn't she talk? Where was Jill's Place? Who was Jill? *Oh, Jill's Place, Jill's Place in the mall.* That was their favorite store. When was she supposed to meet her? Maybe she wanted her to come right away. Whatever, it must be important. She would go right away.

Shay walked down through the mall, still wondering what was going on. She came up to Jill's Place and looked inside. Sue was not in there. In fact, the store was empty except for one lone clerk. She decided to go in and look around and wait for Sue to come, if this was the right time. She was looking at a rack of skirts with her back to the door when behind her, she heard Sue say, "Don't turn around. I think I am being followed. I've got some information I think you might be interested in." Shay could hear the hangers squeaking as Sue slid them along the clothes bar. "It's in the jacket pocket here." She heard Sue move to another rack.

Shay worked her way around to the other side of the rack she was looking at. When she looked up, Sue was just walking out of the store. Shay went to the rack Sue had been looking at, and on the third jacket, she felt something in the pocket. It felt like several sheets of paper folded up. She took them out and slipped them in her purse. She browsed several more racks before leaving the store.

When Shay came out of Jill's Place, she looked both directions to see if anybody was watching her. She didn't see anybody, but that didn't mean there wasn't somebody. She went in several other stores and finally left the mall. When she got to her car, she locked all the doors before backing out of her parking space. As she left the mall parking lot, she kept looking in the mirror to make sure nobody was following her. After several turns onto different streets and she was sure there was nobody behind her, she pulled into a MacDonald's fast food and parked. Checking to make sure the doors were still locked, she took the folded papers out of her purse.

There was a note from Sue and a copy of an e-mail. The e-mail was from Jippem to Barry.

> *Barry,*
>
> *Have you got the Z bar 3 deal tied up yet? It is of the utmost importance that we get this closed, one way or other, as soon as possible. Rhodes insists that we get rid of the cash at once.*
>
> *There is another shipment coming in on Thursday. We need that airstrip now!*
>
> *Jip*

How in the world did Sue get a copy of this e-mail? No wonder she was afraid somebody was following her. She sure didn't want to get Sue in trouble. Then she read the note from Sue.

> *Shay,*
>
> *I shouldn't have this e-mail, but I knew you had to see it. I went in the office the other night to get some papers I needed the next morning. Barry's radio was playing, and I went in to turn it off for him. The e-mail was lying on top of some papers on his desk, and I made a copy of it. I'm not sure what it means, but it looks like something fishy is going on.*
>
> *I guess I have been asking too many questions. That's why I feel my phone may be tapped, and I may be followed.*
>
> *The only way I will contact you from now on is by mail sent to Post Office Box 648, 18-37-9. You can use the same box.*
>
> *Be careful!*
>
> *Sue*

Shay went right to the post office and sent what she got from Sue, along with a note of her own by registered mail to Dallas.

Dallas,

I don't want to have these notes with me, but I thought you should see them.

Shay

Two days after Barry Killmee and his partner were out to the ranch, Dallas got the letter from Shay. What was going on? Not only did Barry vow to get even, but now Shay was in the middle of it as well. He would call her and tell her to leave it alone and maybe even go to her folks' place in Texas. The last thing he wanted was for Shay to get hurt.

No he couldn't call her. What if somebody had tapped her phone? He would drop her a note to P.O. Box 648.

Shay,
Please come to the ranch at once! I need to know that you are safe!
Dallas

And he sent it the same day.

CHAPTER TWELVE

Dallas had just poured himself a cup of coffee and sat down at the kitchen table to rest for a minute or two. He had a lot on his mind, the mortgage was due in a few days, Jippem had called again to see if he could talk him into selling, they were about out of hay, and the pasture was drying up. *Lord what are we going to do?* he said to the Lord and to himself. No matter how much he prayed, he didn't get a clear answer.

About that time, he heard a truck tear into the yard, its horn a blaring. *What is going on?* he asked himself as he jumped up and went to the back door. Hank threw open the door and hollered, "FIRE, FIRE, FIRE!"

"Where?"

"Over in the west pasture and coming this way like crazy."

"Get a hold of all the men on the radio and tell them to get back here fast."

"Joe," Dallas hollered, "start the pumps and fill all the stock tanks! Is Pedro around?"

"Yes, he's in the barn."

"Tell him to hook up the tractor to the disk and disk around all the buildings."

"Is the water truck full of water?"

"Yes, I think so," said Hank, "but I'll check."

About that time, two more pickups came tearing up the road, and Dallas recognized them as a couple of neighbors.

"What can we do? We saw the smoke and came as quick as we could."

"One of you go up to the Millers and tell them to get out of there. If you have time and can get that tractor started, plow around the buildings. Ralph, why don't you take the water truck up there and see what you can do? If it gets too hot, get out of there."

Dallas got on another tractor and made a couple of circles around the airplane hangars and then started disking up and down the main road from the buildings to the gate and back again. If nothing else, with a wide enough fire brake, they maybe could stop the fire there. He could see to the west that the smoke was black and getting bigger. The wind had calmed some, but the fire was still moving mighty fast. From where he was working, he could see more people coming, and he saw the flashing red lights of the Tumble Weed fire trucks followed by another fire department from somewhere. He was almost out to the main gate with the tractor and disk when he saw a wall of flames come up over the hill. All at once, the noise of his tractor was drowned out by a terrible roar of four Pratt and Whitney R-1830 engines on a modified World War II B-24 Liberator. It came in low and dropped a two-thousand-gallon mixture of water and fire retardant, knocking out the main flame.

Grady Kraft, the chief of the Tumble Weed Fire Department, hollered, "Move in fast and put out the smaller fires before the wind turns them into a torrent again!" The bomber pilot used all of its fifty-four hundred horse power to climb out, make a turn, and get ready for another pass to drop another part of his load. Just then, a call came in over the radio, "Guys, I'm in trouble. I'm right in front of a big flaming wall, and I buried the water truck in a soft spot in the field."

"Stay in the truck!" Grady hollered over the radio. "I repeat, stay in the truck."

Grady switched frequencies and said, "This is Fire Chief Grady Kraft calling the water bomber. Do you read me? Over."

"Fire bomber, we read you, over."

"I've got one of my men stuck in a small water truck in the heavy flames to the south, over."

"I see him. Tell him to stay in the truck. The retardant will protect him."

Grady switched back to the first frequency. "Jim, stay in the truck. Say again, stay in the truck. Do you read? Over."

"I read you. I'm in the truck, but it's getting hot, over!"

"The B-24 is going to bomb you, over."

As Grady switched back to the bomber frequency, he saw the plane come in low and slow, drop his load, and disappear into the wall of smoke. Over the radio he heard, "We hit him dead center. Get some men down there and quick."

The crop duster from across the river came in and made several passes with his 602 Ag-Tractor, dumping loads of water on the smaller flames around the water truck Jim was in.

Dallas turned around and disked down the other side of the drive back to the house and up around the buildings again. The fire had cut around and was almost to the river. That was when he saw a helicopter, with a large bucket hanging below it, drop a payload of water on the north side of the fire. This cut the fire off from going up past the buildings. The helicopter headed back to the river to get another load. He worked back and forth until he had the fire completely cut off to the north. He found out later it was a Blackhawk helicopter from the South Dakota National Guard. Now the only direction the fire was going was to the south. There were few roads down in that part of the ranch, and the only way it could be put out was with the water bomber. In places, they couldn't keep up to the fire with a four-wheel-drive truck. The fire was moving so fast. As it got dark, the planes and the helicopter had to quit flying, but the wind also went down, so the fire didn't move as fast. Crews worked far into the night to put out the smaller fires and make sure the hot spots were out. Women from town and the neighboring ranches made lunches and brought them out to the men along with water and coffee.

By noon the next day, things were pretty well under control, and the men, who had worked for twenty-four to thirty hours, found places in the bunkhouse or one of the barns to get a quick nap. Others, like Hank and Dallas, had a bite to eat and headed right back out, checking hot spots and fence posts that were still burning. A mile or so from the main house, they met the ranch water truck coming with two men. One was driving, and the other was riding on top spraying smoldering spots as they came.

Dallas and Hank pulled up and stopped. "How you guys doing?" he hollered.

"Good, we got everything to the west, but we're about out of water."

"Everything between here and the buildings looks good," said Dallas. "You guys wouldn't like some water and a sandwich, would you?"

"Hey, that's great," said Joe, climbing down off the top of the truck.

"How about you, cowboy?" Dallas walked over to the cab of the water wagon. "Shay! What are you doing here? I thought I told all the women to leave."

"Since when did I have to take orders from you? I'm a better truck driver than any of the guys you have working for you, except maybe Joe here."

"She's right, Mr. Z. She took this rig through places I'd never try to go."

"Well, I still don't like it. This fire was way too dangerous."

"Dallas, I wasn't trying to please you. I was trying to put out some fire, and if you ask me, I think we did a pretty good job. What do you say, Joe?" She turned to her partner.

"You're right, ma'am."

"You amaze me, Shay. I've never seen a woman like you," he said softly so the other two couldn't hear.

"I was just doing what had to be done."

"What are you doing out here anyway?"

"Remember, you told me in your note to please come to the ranch?" She walked back to the truck and got in.

"I guess we're moving," said Joe, and he climbed back up on the truck.

When Dallas and Hank got back to the ranch, he noticed that Shay's car was still there, but she was nowhere in sight. He went in the house and asked Martha if she had seen Shay.

"Yes, she's here. I got her some clean clothes and sent her upstairs to shower and get some sleep. She's been going since she came early yesterday morning."

"Yesterday morning?! You knew she was here?"

"Yes, open your eyes, you big blockhead. She loves you, and she wasn't going to leave you when there was something she could do to help."

"Oh, she doesn't love me. Besides, she could have been hurt. I'd kill myself if anything happened that would harm her."

"Well, don't waste the bullets. I'm okay."

Dallas whirled around. There stood Shay taking in everything he had said.

"I think it is time for me to leave," said Martha as she walked out with a grin on her face and a twinkle in her eye.

Dallas just stood there with his mouth open. He didn't know what to say. Shay had her hair pulled back in a ponytail and had on big round gold wire earrings, blue jeans, boots, and a long-sleeved Western shirt with the collar turned up. She wore just a touch of makeup and a big smile on her face.

"You clean up pretty good," he finally blurted out.

"My, you're good with words! I wished I could say the same for you. Look at you—you're a mess." He looked at his hands and shirt. They were both black.

"Look in the mirror," she said, and she pointed at one hanging on the wall above one of the cabinets. He looked up and started to laugh. A tuft of hair was standing straight on end, and he had a black moustache where he must have rubbed his nose. One eye was all black, and his left cheek was covered with soot. He didn't know if he would ever get his clothes clean. He may just have to throw them away.

"Maybe I should at least wash my face." They both laughed. "Maybe I should take a shower. What do you think?"

"Yes, I think so, with your clothes on."

"I'm going to wipe off my face and then go out and thank the neighbors and make sure they all got something to eat."

As Dallas walked down the walk, a truck with three guys was just leaving.

"Hey, thanks, guys!"

"Glad to help, you'd do the same for us. When you find out the damage, let us know. We'll give you a hand putting things back together." With that, they waved and drove off.

Dallas walked around and thanked and talked to different groups. Some were getting into their pickups, and others were just standing around, talking and finishing the last of their coffee. He put his arm around some of the ladies from church who had worked so hard preparing food for all who worked. He went over and talked to the men from the National Guard while they were finishing their lunch. A lot of the men had gone without sleep for thirty-six hours. He talked to Grady and the firemen from Tumble Weed and thanked them for all the time they put in on the fire too. Shay stood on the porch and watched Dallas make the rounds. She could tell the people really liked this guy, and she was proud of him. She saw the sheriff motion for Dallas to come over to his car, and they talked for quite a while.

Gretchen walked up to where Shay was standing, "How you doing, Shay?"

"I'm doing okay."

"What are you doing out here?"

"I just came to help."

"You look tired, Gretchen. You want to come in and clean up a little before you go home?"

"Naw, I'm okay. Are you going to marry Mr. Z?"

"No, we're just friends. Where did you get that idea?"

"You're so pretty. If Mr. Z. doesn't marry, you he must be blind."

"Pretty is only skin deep. Real pretty is on the inside."

"I wish I was pretty like you. The boys don't even look at me. We had a basket social at church last year, and Dallas bought mine, but I know my dad asked him to."

"Have they set the date for the next one?"

"Yes, in a couple of weeks."

"Remember, you and I are going shopping for a new dress, and we'll knock the socks of those guys."

"You remembered," said Gretchen. "I thought you might forget."

"Not on your life! It will be fun, and I'm looking forward to it."

"Oh thanks, you are the best." And she turned and ran down the steps to her truck.

"What in the world did you say to her? When she went by me, she was ten feet off the ground. I said hi, and she didn't even answer me," Dallas commented as he walked up to Shay.

"Never mind, it was just girl talk."

"Well, I think everybody is gone. I'm going to take a shower."

"Take it down in the utility room. No use getting your bath upstairs all dirty. I laid out some clothes for you."

Dallas looked at her with a strange look on his face. "How did you know where my clothes were?"

"Martha told me."

"It's bad enough having one woman in the house telling me what to do. Now we have two."

"Yes, you do, and I don't like your attitude. You better shape up."

Dallas was scrubbing away when he heard somebody close the washer door. "Who goes there?"

"Just me, I'm washing your clothes for Martha."

"Doesn't a guy get any privacy around here?"

"Not during working hours, we all have to get our work done."

"You've been around Martha too long. I can see that."

He got out of the shower and put on the clothes Shay had laid out for him and walked into the kitchen.

"Wow, you do clean up pretty well yourself."

"Where did you get these clothes? This isn't one of my shirts."

"I know. I picked it up for your birthday. Do you like it?"

"It's not my birthday."

"I know it's not until next week, but . . ."

"How do you know that?"

"Martha said so."

"Martha talks too much."

"Dallas, you told me to tell Shay when your birthday was so she would be sure and buy you a present," said Martha who was standing in the doorway, listening to their conversation.

"I did not, but I like it, thank you."

"Sit down," said Martha. "Have a cup of coffee and a piece of my fresh apple pie."

About that time, Hank walked in, "Well, well, some of us are out working, and some of us are in the house eating pie."

"Oh, sit down before your pie gets cold," barked Martha.

"Say, Mr. Z.," said Hank, "how about paying me by the hour instead of the month? I put in a week in the last two days."

"Good idea, then this winter when you're sitting in the house on your fanny, you'll get paid for about twelve hours a month."

"Well, we could go back to paying by the month then."

"You two are worse than a couple of kids," said Martha.

"I wonder who started the fire and why," said Hank

"I think I know who and why. You know those two guys who were here last week? They vowed to get even."

"Do you think so," said Shay.

"Yes, I think somebody set it, and so does the sheriff. He was going over to where it started to see if he could find any clues."

"Isn't it illegal to set fires, and couldn't they get in a lot of trouble for doing it?" asked Shay.

"Sure could, especially if that fireman who was caught in the crossfire would have died. He was just lucky he stayed in the truck, and they bombed him with fire retardant in time."

Dallas stretched and said, "I think I'll drive over where the fire started and look around and maybe go by the Miller Place. Somebody said there's nothing left over there."

Hank slid his chair back. "I'll go with you."

"No, you won't. You take a shower and go to bed. On second thought, I don't care if you take a shower or not."

"Neither do I," said Martha, "he can sleep in the barn." Everybody laughed.

Dallas stood up and took his hat off the peg by the door. Shay was right behind him.

"Where do you think you're going?"

"With you."

"No, you're not. You haven't had any sleep either."

"I've had more than you. Besides, I don't work here. I don't have to take orders from you."

"Sounds to me like she's going," said Hank, "and as foreman of this ranch, she has my permission."

"That's all we need around this place—more bosses."

"Come on, big boy." Shay took Dallas by the hand and headed for the door. "The only reason you want to go by yourself is so you can be boss, but when we get out on the range, I promise to do everything you tell me to."

As Hank watched them go hand in hand down the walk and Dallas helped her in his pickup, he said, "Yep, she's got him hooked. All she has to do is reel him in."

"No, Dallas has his head screwed on straight. He'll never marry her until she accepts Christ," said Martha.

"Oh, I know that, but you can't be with Dallas long before she'll want what he has."

Dallas and Shay drove away from the homestead in silence, overlooking the charred black hills. They followed the road around the west side of the ranch. This was where they got the fire stopped. There were a few burnt spots on the other side of the road, but they were small and had been put out quickly.

"Doesn't this just make you sick?" asked Shay.

Dallas didn't answer right away. "Sad, yes. Sick, no. God says in his Word that all things work together for good to them that love the Lord. Well, I love the Lord, so I know that from this fire, something will work out for the good."

"What good could come out of this? What are you going to feed the cows now that the best pasture is gone?"

"Hay, I guess."

"Where are you going to get hay? There's none in the country!"

"I don't know, but God does."

"Oh, so your God is in the hay business now too. If God has so much money, why don't you ask him to pay off your note at the bank?"

"I have."

"I'm sorry. That was uncalled for," said Shay.

"No, that's okay. I've asked the same questions myself."

"You have?"

"Sure, I'm only human, you know."

"Well, why doesn't he?"

"I don't know, but one thing I do know is whatever he has planned for me is good. Maybe he wants me to dig ditches or drive a truck. Maybe he wants me to be the CEO of a Fortune 500 company. Who knows? Whatever it is, there I will be happy."

"Do you really believe all that?"

"You bet I do, with all my heart."

"But look at all this. As far as you can see in every direction is black, burnt, charred, and dead."

"No," said Dallas," under all that blackness are seeds. In a few days, you'll see green poking through everywhere."

"What about the Miller Place? That's all gone."

"That house needed to be replaced anyway, and if I lose the ranch, I won't have to rebuild it."

"You are a crazy optimist. You don't live in the real world. You could have lost all of the ranch buildings including your beautiful house."

"Yes, but did you notice just as that bomber came in to drop his load of fire retardant, the wind stopped? He put out four times as much fire as if the wind would have been blowing. Even the professional firefighters were amazed. That's what saved the buildings and stopped the fire."

"So now you think God controls the wind?"

"Don't you?"

"Okay, I'll give you that one."

"Thank you," he said with a grin.

Up ahead, they could see a car parked, and Dallas recognized it as the sheriff's car.

"Well, here's where it started," said the sheriff as Dallas and Shay walked up. "Wasn't much of a professional job. Whoever it was left a gas can and a book of matches. My brother's here for a week or so. I'll have him sit around a few bars and listen. Somebody is bound to do some talking. This has gotten pretty serious. I just got a call on the radio. One of the firefighters from Foxhome was burnt real badly. He was airlifted to the hospital in Sioux Falls, but they said he died on the way. Now we have a murder on our hands too."

Before they got home, Shay went to sleep. As they bounced down the gravel road, her head fell over onto Dallas's shoulder, and he put his arm around her to make her more comfortable. She awoke just as they were driving up to the main house.

"Do you always go to sleep when you go for a ride in a truck?"

"No, just when they work you all night and all day."

He took his arm from around her.

"Do you always take advantage of a girl when she is sleeping?"

"No, just the ones I want to."

"Oh, are there several?"

"I'll never tell."

CHAPTER THIRTEEN

"You guys go ahead and eat before it gets cold. Hank will be here in a minute," said Martha to Dallas and Shay who were sitting at the kitchen table the morning after the big fire. About that time, Hank came busting through the door. "Did you order a load of hay!" he shouted.

"No."

"Well, there's a guy in a semi, loaded with hay, down by the barn and another one just topped the hill to the west."

Dallas slid his chair back and walked to the kitchen window. Sure enough, there sat a semi. A second semi was just pulling in the yard.

"Yep," he said, "I guess God is in the hay business." He looked at Shay.

"Right," said Shay, "you had me there for a bit."

Dallas didn't answer but grabbed his jacket and hat and followed Hank out the door. Shay was right behind them. As they walked up to the truck, the driver was just climbing down from the cab.

"Morning, fellows, you guys need hay?"

"Yes, we sure do, but who sent you?"

"God."

"God?"

"Yes, sir, I had these two loads of hay loaded for a customer in Iowa, and God told me last night that somebody in South Dakota needed it worse than the farmer in Iowa. I told the other driver to follow me. He asked where we were going, and I told him I didn't know. So we headed out with God telling me where to turn and what roads to take, and here we are. I don't know where we are or who you are, but I know I did what God told me to do."

"Well, praise the Lord! We just got through putting out a fire that destroyed a lot of our pasture and what little hay we had. I didn't know what we were going to feed our cattle this morning. I'm Dallas Ziglar, and this is my foreman, Hank Olson." He stuck out his hand.

"I'm Joe Gustafson. and this is one of my good men, Sam Johnson. We're from Minnesota, south of Mankato.

"Come on in, guys. Let's have some breakfast before we unload that hay."

"Shay, tell Martha—" he started to say as he turned around, but Shay was just going up the steps of the ranch house.

"I don't believe it," said Shay as she came into the kitchen. Martha was frying some more eggs. "Dallas told me God would provide, but I didn't know he hauled hay. What can I help you with, Martha?" she asked.

"Just believe, but for now, you can make some toast and set some more places. How many are there?"

"Just two, I think."

As the guys walked in the door, Martha and Shay were just putting the last of the food on the table. Bacon, eggs, fried potatoes, pancakes, toast, and plenty of hot coffee made up the meal.

"Man, this is better than Perkins! You guys sure have some good wives."

"No, no, don't get me married off! These two are bossy. This is Martha, Hank's wife, and this is a friend, Shay. Shay, Joe Gustafson and Sam Johnson," he said pointing at the two guys.

"Sit, eat," said Martha, "if this ain't the way you want your eggs, you can go to the restaurant. It's only about thirty-five miles."

"See what I mean?"

"Let's go, Mr. Z.," said Hank as he started to slide his chair back. "Maybe the service will be a little better too."

"The service matches the tips," chimed in Shay.

"I guess I will stay," said Dallas. "Let's ask the blessing."

"Dear Lord," started Dallas, "we come before you this morning with humble hearts. We thank you for Joe and Sam and their willingness to follow your leading. We also thank you for watching out for us your servants and providing for us in this our time of need. We thank you for your protection during the fire and for saving our buildings and loved ones. We also thank you for all the help you supplied from neighbors and firemen. We thank you for this breakfast that we are about to partake of. Bless Martha and Shay for all the work they've put into this meal. We love you and will do our best to serve you. Amen."

"Amen," said Joe.

Shay looked at Dallas with tears in her eyes, and their eyes met. *What a man!* she thought to herself. They started to pass the food around while Martha set a pan of hot caramel rolls in the center of the table, which she had just taken out of the oven.

"I don't know about you two guys," said Joe, "but I think you better hang on to these two women."

"That's what we've been trying to tell them," said Shay, and she looked at Dallas. He smiled.

"Yeah, I guess I will," added Hank. "New ones are hard to train. I've been working on this one for almost forty years."

"More coffee?" asked Shay as she came to the table with a coffeepot.

"Just exactly where are we?" asked Sam.

"You are at the Z bar 3 Ranch, four miles on the other side of nowhere."

"I can believe that," said Joe. "I'm not sure I can find my way out of here."

"God led you here. I guess he can get you out. If not, I can draw you a map," said Dallas with a grin.

"Did you guys drive all night?" asked Hank.

"Yep, we left about nine last night."

"That's the exact time you told me God would provide," said Shay.

They sat around and shot the breeze for a while after they finished their breakfast, getting to know each other a little better, while Martha and Shay cleaned off the table and started doing dishes.

"Martha, show these guys the guest rooms," Dallas said. "You guys get some sleep while Hank and I get the men to unload those trucks. Hand me my checkbook over there, will you, Shay? How much do I owe you?"

"Don't know," said Joe. "God ain't told me yet. When he does, I'll send you a bill."

"No, really." Dallas laughed. "How much?"

"You know, Dallas, God owns the cattle on a thousand hills. He just told me to feed some of them for him."

"Sam, how much is hay going for in Minnesota?"

"I don't know. I learned a long time ago not to get between God and Joe."

"No, please, Dallas, don't steal God's blessing from me. I don't know who you are or where you live. All I know is you must be one of God's children, and he's letting me help take care of you. I'll let God pay me. He always does a real good job."

Dallas handed the checkbook back to Shay with tears in his eyes but never said a thing.

"Thanks for that good breakfast, dear," said Hank as he got up from the table. "You're a good woman. I'll get the guys unloading that hay," he said as he left the kitchen.

"Come on, men," said Martha. "I'll show you where you can get some sleep. When you get up, we'll have some good food for you."

As Dallas stepped out on the porch, Shay was right behind him. "Dallas,"—he turned around—"who are those guys?"

"I don't know. I've never seen them before in my life."

"Did you order that hay?"

"No, dear, honest." Dallas saw tears in Shay's eyes as she turned and went back in the house.

"What's wrong, dear?" asked Martha.

"That man, I wish I could believe like he does."

"You can, my dear, read John 3:16."

Martha said no more. She didn't have to. The Lord would take care of it. He was dealing with Shay, and she was thinking.

By the time Dallas got out to the semis, the guys had almost all of the first truck unloaded.

"When you're finished," said Dallas, "pull those trucks over to the fuel barrel and fill the tanks."

"How do you want us to feed the cattle, Mr. Z?" asked Pedro. "Most of the cattle are in the north pasture, but there are some way down south. I don't know if they'll cross where the fire was or not."

"Let's just leave them there. They have water, don't they?"

"Yeah, they can get down to the river."

"Well, let's just haul some hay down to them."

"They won't need too much. There's still some grass down there."

"The ones up north," Dallas continued, "we should scatter hay in several places for them."

By lunchtime, the cattle were taken care of, and the cowboys were riding the south pasture to see how many, if any, cattle were lost in the fire.

Dallas and Hank were just heading to the house for lunch when they saw Joe and Sam come out on the porch. Shay was right behind them. "The quicker you wash up, the quicker you can eat. Martha just put the steaks on the grill, and they'll be done in a few minutes. How do you guys like your steaks?" she asked and looked at Joe and Sam.

"Medium well," said Joe.

"That's fine for me too," added Sam.

"I want mine—" said Dallas.

"I know how you want yours," cut in Shay. One thing about it, Martha liked to cook, and with Shay's help, they really put on a feed.

"Another piece of pie?" asked Shay.

"No," said Joe, "we've only been here for two meals and already I've put on ten pounds."

"We don't want you to tell your wives that we didn't take good care of you while you were here," added Shay.

"Make me a promise," said Dallas, "that you will come back with your wives. There's real good fishing on the river here, and we'll show you what ranch life is really like."

"We'll do that. Both our wives would really like it out here. It's so peaceful."

"We better get on the road. We've got a few miles before we get home. Then we'll have to load and get some hay to that farmer in Iowa before the weekend."

"You don't know how much I appreciate getting this hay. I know the Lord will bless you for all you've done."

Everybody walked the guys out to their trucks. After saying their good-byes, they were ready to get in their cabs to leave.

"How much diesel do you have, Sam?" asked Joe.

"I don't know. Let me look." He climbed up into his truck and started it, then opened the door, and hollered, "I'm full!"

"Is that gauge acting up again? Let me see how much I have."

Joe took a look and said, "I'm full too."

"Looks like God is in the fuel business too," said Dallas with a grin on his face.

"Thanks, guys!" And they waved as they pulled out of the yard.

Martha and Hank went back in the house. The rest of the cowboys went back to what they were doing. Dallas and Shay stood and watched the last of the dust settle as the semis drove out of sight. Shay reached over and took Dallas's hand and said, "How did you know they would come with the hay?"

"I didn't. I was just as surprised as you were when I saw those two trucks pull into the yard. I knew God would take care of us. I just didn't know how he was going to do it."

"Didn't you lie awake all night worrying about it?"

"No, why should I? I gave it to the Lord. He was going to be up all night anyway."

"Dallas, I can't understand you. You always look on the bright side of things."

"Not always, Shay, sometimes I even question God. In the next few weeks, I have to come up with the mortgage payment or lose the ranch. I've prayed about it but don't seem to get any answers. I know God will work it out for the best, but I still get impatient. I'm human you know."

"I wish I could have the faith you have."

CHAPTER FOURTEEN

It was a warm sunny afternoon when Gretchen met Shay in Rapid City. She was dressed in her cowgirl attire with blue jeans and boots. She had driven her old pickup truck all the way, and Shay was surprised that it made the trip.

"Have you had anything to eat today?" Shay asked.

"Yeah, I stopped at MacDonald's just as I came into town."

"Have you been to Rapid very much?"

"Once or twice."

"Well, let's go. We'll take my car." Shay spent the next couple of hours showing Gretchen different things around town, and when she was through, she took her to a nice restaurant for dinner. After they finished eating, they went to a movie that neither one of them had seen before. It was quite late when they finally got back to Shay's condo.

"I can't remember having this much fun," said Gretchen.

"That was fun," admitted Shay, "but we better get some sleep. We want to get an early start shopping in the morning." Shay showed Gretchen to her guestroom.

"This is so nice," she said. "I would like a pretty room like this."

"Good night, friend, see you in the morning." Shay closed the door.

Shay was asleep almost before her head hit the pillow and didn't wake up until she heard some movement in the bathroom. *What is that?* she thought, and then it dawned on her that Gretchen was in the guestroom.

She looked at the clock; six fifteen. This was as bad as staying at the ranch. Doesn't anybody sleep in anymore?" Shay reluctantly rolled out of bed and stumbled into the kitchen. There was Gretchen fixing coffee.

"Morning, Shay, it's such a nice morning. I hope I didn't wake you."

"No," Shay lied, "it was time to get up anyway. Well, let's get shopping. We're going to have to hurry to get this all done and make it to the party tonight. We'll grab some breakfast on the way." Then she thought to herself, *What stores are open this time of the day?* They would have to kill some time at breakfast, and then Jill would be in her shop a little before eight.

"It shouldn't take to long just to buy a dress, will it?"

"Oh, we are going all the way. We are going to make a new woman out of you. I'm so excited. First, we're going to stop at my girlfriend's shop and give you a new hairdo. Then we'll go dress shopping. This is going to be so much fun!"

"I don't know if I have enough money for all of that."

"Don't worry about it. I have friends that owe me, and the rest I will pay for. We are going to make those guys pay for the privilege of eating with you tonight. I know one of the guys that work at the Z bar 3 has had his eye on you for a long time. He's been too shy to ask you for a date, but he's going to wish he had asked you sooner before some other guy snatched you up."

"Who?" Gretchen asked, starting to blush.

"Oh, I can't tell you, but you'll find out tonight. When we're done, you'll be able to drive him crazy."

"Do you think so?"

"You just wait and see," said Shay.

The new hairdo took a couple of hours while the three of them talked and laughed as they worked. When they turned the chair around and Gretchen looked at herself in the mirror, her mouth dropped open. She couldn't believe her eyes!

"What do you think?" asked Shay.

"That doesn't even look like me! Nobody will know who I am, but I like it."

"That's good. We want to surprise everybody. Just wait until we're done!" Shay and Jill checked for just the right colors, and then they put on a little makeup and some dangle earrings. "There, that should drive the guys nuts. They're going to wish they had paid more attention to you sooner." Gretchen turned her head from side to side as she looked herself over in the mirror.

"Is that really me?" she asked.

"Yes, it is, and you're so pretty," said Jill.

"I like it," said Gretchen. "I've never had my hair fixed in a beauty shop before."

"You two have fun," Jill said as they left her shop. "I wish I could go with you guys, but I can't leave the shop."

"Don't I have to pay her?" asked Gretchen.

"No, she owes me one. Besides, she had a lot of fun doing it. Now to the shoe store."

"Oh, I've got shoes."

"Not like the ones we're going to buy." They went into a shoe store in the mall, and Shay picked out some white high heels and said, "Try these on." Shay had a hard time to keep from laughing as Gretchen tried to take the first few steps.

"How do you walk in these things anyway?" she asked.

"Oh, you'll get use to them. By the end of the day, you'll have it down pat and will be able to run and dance in them. You have to wear high heels. They make your legs look longer."

Shortly after lunch, Gretchen stepped out of a dressing room and spun around in front of a full-length mirror.

"That's it! That's it!" cried Shay. "Wow, you're so pretty. The guys will be fighting over you. Let's go. I want to stop by my place and change into a dress." It didn't take Shay long, and she was just fixing her hair when Gretchen said that they better get going, or they would be late.

"Oh, you want to be slightly late. Come in ten minutes after it's started. We want to make sure everybody is there. We want you to make a grand entrance."

"Oh, this is so crazy. I'll be so embarrassed."

"No, you'll do just fine. Now, when someone says you look so nice, don't blush. Just say thank you. Some of the girls are going to be jealous and maybe say some mean things—just smile. Now let's practice."

"Gretchen, is that you? Wow, you look nice."

"Do you think so?"

"No, say, 'Why, thank you.' Let's try again. Gretchen, my, you look nice."

'Why, thank you."

"*Good*, that is such a pretty dress."

"Why, thank you."

"Did you get all dolled up to steal my man?"

Gretchen just smiled.

"Good, now remember those things."

It took them a little over three hours to drive back to Tumble Weed. Shay was ahead, and Gretchen followed in her pickup truck. When they got within a couple of miles of the church, Shay pulled off the road and Gretchen stopped behind her. Shay got out and walked back to where she was parked.

"You take my car from here. You're too beautiful to arrive in a truck."

"But what about you?"

"I'll take your pickup. This is your night." Shay looked at her watch. "It's almost seven. You wait here until ten minutes after and then you come. Now remember, no matter what anybody says, smile and say, 'Why thank you.' You got it?"

"Yes, but I'm so nervous."

"You'll do just fine. Remember you're a new woman."

Shay soon arrived at the church and walked up to where Dallas was standing in the church fellowship hall. "How's it going?" she asked.

"Good, things are just getting started. I wasn't sure you were coming."

"Oh, I wouldn't miss it for anything."

"Did you bring your basket?"

"Yes, I got my secret peanut butter and jelly recipe."

"You mean I have to pay twenty bucks for a peanut-butter-and-jelly sandwich?"

"Is that all you would pay to eat with me?"

"Oh, I might go twenty-one fifty."

They turned back to what was going on with the auction just as the auctioneer said, "Sold to Jim Brown for forty dollars!" Everyone clapped. "That's the highest bid so far," said the auctioneer.

"How about this young lady that's just coming in?"

Gretchen greeted several people as she walked toward the stage, and Shay read her lips as she said, "Why, thank you."

Joe, one of the ranch hands standing by the door, pointed at her as she walked by and said to Rusty, "Is that Gretchen? What a knockout!"

Dallas leaned over and said to Shay, "Who is that?"

"How should I know? You're the one who's dated all the women in the county."

"Not that one, I haven't."

"You probably have and forgot it."

Gretchen walked up on the stage, her full skirt swishing around her legs. She was carrying a small picnic basket with a bow matching her dress on the handle.

113

"Who'll start the bidding?"

"Fifty bucks," said Joe by the door and started toward the stage to claim his prize.

"I have fifty," said the auctioneer. "Who'll give me fifty-five?"

"Fifty-five," rang out from the back.

Joe stopped and looked around to see who was bidding.

"Fifty-five, who'll make it sixty?"

"Sixty," said Joe.

"Sixty, I've got sixty. Who'll give sixty-five?"

Joe, who was on his way to claim Gretchen, looked around as the auctioneer took another bid for sixty-five.

"I've got sixty-five. Who'll give me seventy?"

"Seventy," hollered Dallas.

Shay elbowed him in the ribs. "What are you doing? I thought you only had twenty bucks."

"Seventy, thank you. I need seventy-five."

Joe was back talking to Rusty, and Rusty was laughing.

Shay watched as she saw Rusty hand Joe a twenty. He counted his money. Turning around, he held up his hand and hollered, "One hundred and twenty-five!"

The auctioneer stopped for a minute and looked at Joe. "I have one hundred twenty-five. Going once, going twice, sold to Mr. Joe Sandford for one hundred twenty-five dollars. Thank you!" Everybody applauded as he went to the stage to claim Gretchen. He took her by the hand and led her to the back of the auditorium as several people greeted them and patted Joe on the back. They auctioned off several more, and finally the auctioneer said, "How about this young lady standing by Mr. Ziglar?" Shay walked up to the front.

"Okay, let's start the bidding with twenty dollars. I have twenty. Who'll give me twenty-five?"

"Two hundred!" yelled Dallas.

"Man, you must know what's in that basket," said the auctioneer and everybody laughed.

"She told me it was peanut butter and jelly."

Everybody roared.

"Two hundred once, two hundred twice—"

"Two fifty," said Shay.

The auctioneer looked at Shay in surprise. "The lady bids two hundred fifty. It appears she don't want to eat with you, Dallas."

Again the crowd roared with laughter.

"Three hundred."

"Good, good, I have three hundred. Do I hear three fifty?"

Shay raised her hand.

"Three fifty?" asked the auctioneer. Shay nodded. "I have three hundred and fifty. Who will give me four hundred?"

"Four!" hollered Dallas.

"I have four hundred. Who will give me four fifty?" And the auctioneer looked at Shay.

"Oh, let him have it. I guess I could put up with him for half an hour for four hundred dollars," said Shay. Dallas headed for the stage. Shay held out her hand to him, but he ignored it and picked her up in his arms, whirled her around a couple of times, and carried her to the back of the room. The whole crowd was on their feet, laughing and clapping as they went. They all knew the money was going to pay for the new fellowship hall they were going to build. Dallas carried Shay over to the table where Joe and Gretchen were sitting and set her down.

Shay turned to Gretchen and said, "What are you doing getting my man to bid on you and your basket?"

Gretchen just smiled and said, "Why, thank you!"

"Gretchen, is that you? You look so nice!" said Dallas.

"Why, thank you. That's Ms. Olson to you."

"That's good," said Shay as she patted Gretchen's arm. "Put these men in their place."

"If I would've known that was you, I'd have bid more."

"You leave my girl alone, Mr. Z. She cost me a hundred and twenty-five dollars."

"Oh, Joe, I'll pay you back," said Gretchen.

"No, Gretchen, you don't pay him back. You tell him if he's going to keep you, he'll have to spend a lot more than a hundred twenty-five bucks. Good women cost money."

"Boy, you can say that again. Look what it cost me," said Joe.

"Okay, I'm not going to pay you back."

"You shouldn't complain, Joe," said Dallas. "I'll have to sell my truck to pay for this woman, but she's worth it."

"You better add that," said Shay.

A few more baskets and the auction was over, and everyone sat around enjoying the lunches the women had prepared. There was a lot of talking and laughing. It wasn't hard to tell that everyone was having a good time, and by the size of the crowd, there was no question that the church needed a bigger fellowship hall. Before anybody left, the pastor got up and said, "I have an announcement to make. Thanks to all you, good people, we raised twenty four hundred, sixty-three dollars and fifty cents. Thanks to Paul Carter for raising his bid three dollars and fifty cents. Everyone applauded and laughed at the same time.

As they walked out of the fellowship hall, Dallas threw his keys to Joe. "Take my truck and see that Gretchen gets home. I'm going with Shay."

"What makes you think I'm going to the ranch?" Shay asked.

"What other motel do you have to stay at? Besides, I need to get some of my money back. Poolside rooms are two hundred twenty-five dollars a night," Dallas replied.

"You don't even have a pool."

"No, but if you'll stay, I'll build one."

She laid her hand on his, and tenderness passed between them, but neither one said anything.

After a while, Shay said, "That was a lot of fun. I can't remember enjoying myself more. Maybe there is something to this religion."

"It's not religion. That's boring. It's a personal relationship with Jesus Christ."

"Whatever it is, you're different than most guys I know."

When they got home, Martha and Hank were already there, sitting around the table and having a cup of coffee.

"Do we have any rooms left?"

"Oh, I think so," said Martha.

"This young lady needs a room. Put her in the most expensive one we have, and make sure you get cash. Don't take her check."

"You sound a little bitter. Did she call your bluff tonight at the party?"

"That's the way these hotshots from the city are. They come flashing their cash around, and then when it comes right down to business, they quit bidding. I would have bid a lot more if she hadn't quit."

"Just how much would a country boy pay for a city girl?"

"I don't know," said Hank. "It cost me fifty years of hard work, but it was worth it."

"You better add that," grinned Martha. Then she turned to Shay and said, "Was that your idea to fix up Gretchen like that?"

"Yes, I was talking to her after the fire the other night, and she said none of the boys even looked at her. She was afraid nobody would even bid on her basket. I felt so sorry for her. She's such a sweet girl. So she came into Rapid City last night and stayed with me overnight, and this morning we started shopping. First, we went to a hairdresser friend of mine. I told her to give Gretchen the kind of hairdo that would look the best. You should have seen Gretchen's face the first time she saw herself in the mirror. It was worth all the work we put into it. Next, we went to a shoe store and got some high heels. It was so funny. She could hardly walk in them. We laughed and laughed, but I made her wear them all day, and she got really good at it. Then we went dress shopping. That was so much fun. I don't think she even owns a dress."

"No," said Martha, "I've never seen her in one. She hasn't even had a chance to buy one. Living alone with her dad and no mother and her grandpa sure wasn't any help. He would never see why a woman had to dress up for anything."

"When I saw her in that dress she wore tonight, I knew we had hit the jackpot. And pantyhose, I doubt if she's ever worn a pair before. And her bra; I said, 'Throw that thing away, girl. Let's get something lacy and pretty,' and we got her several pairs of panties too. She was just like a little girl at Christmastime. She told me she had never felt like a woman before."

"Bless you, girl," said Martha. "Her father couldn't and wouldn't do what you did for her today. You turned her from a plain teenager into a beautiful woman."

"It was so much fun," said Shay.

"Do you know the most important thing you did for her?" asked Dallas.

"No."

"You gave her self-esteem and confidence. When she walked in tonight, she carried herself with pride and poise. Her dad didn't even know who she was. Did you see the proud look on his face when it finally dawned on him who she was?"

"That's what I told her. Beauty is only skin deep. Real beauty is on the inside."

"Naw," said Dallas, "if I had to choose between marrying a pretty girl or a smart one, I'd marry the pretty one every time."

"You would not," said Shay.

"Yes, I would. A pretty girl you can always send to school to get smart, but you can't do much about a smart homely one."

"Dallas, you are terrible."

Hank and Martha busted out laughing.

"You noticed I only bid on the cute ones tonight."

"That's the trouble with you guys. You bid on the cute ones, but you never quite get your money's worth."

"Oh, I'm not complaining. I think I got more than my money's worth. I would've paid a lot more."

"Why, thank you." She smiled at him. "That's what I told Gretchen to say tonight. No matter what people said to her, just smile and say, 'Why, thank you.'"

"You know, Joe has had his eye on Gretchen for a long time but didn't have the nerve to ask her for a date. Tonight when he saw how beautiful she was, he must have thought if he didn't get her tonight, somebody else would," said Dallas.

Hank slid his chair back. "You guys can sit up all night and talk if you want to, but I've got a job and I have to get up in the morning."

"Me too," said Martha, and they went down the hall holding hands.

"Will you be that much in love when you're their age?" asked Shay.

"I hope so, if you will let me." And he took her by the hand. "Let's sit in the great room where it's more comfortable." They sat down on one of the couches, and Dallas turned on the gas fireplace with the remote control to make it more romantic.

"Shay, I'm so proud of you."

"Why?"

"You took a girl that was snooty to you and chewed you out the first time she met you and helped her become a beautiful woman that she can be proud of. You didn't get mad at her or try to put her down, but because you made her a better woman, that makes you a better, more loving woman."

"Why, thank you." She grinned. "I just thought if you were going to chase her, I better fix her up."

"Shay, don't say that," he said seriously. "I don't need any more woman than the one I am trying to get. She's hard enough to handle."

"I'm sorry. I was just teasing, and I don't want you to be looking around, okay?"

"Okay."

They talked far into the night about the party, the church, the ranch, and the Lord. Neither wanted to go to bed, but they knew they had to or they would never get up in the morning. Shay looked at her watch, "Dallas! It's two o'clock. We have to go to bed." They heard Joe drive in and stop out front of the house. A couple of minutes later, there was a light tap on the door. Dallas went and opened the door.

"I hope it's not too late, but I saw the light on, and I thought you might still be up."

"Is there any gas left in the truck?" asked Dallas.

"Yes," Joe said with a question in his voice.

"Oh," said Dallas, "I thought you must've driven a long way as long as it took you to get home!" He grinned. Joe's face started turning red.

"Is Ms. Shay still up?"

"Yes, I'm here." Shay got up from the couch and walked over to the door.

"Gretchen told me how you helped her get so pretty. She was so beautiful tonight. She wasn't shy but was actually proud of herself and fun to be with. I just realized what I had been missing, and I just wanted to thank you for being so good to her."

"Why, thank you, Joe. That's so sweet of you. I really did it for you. She's a very nice girl. Now you be good to her."

"I will, Ms. Shay, and thanks again."

"Good night."

"Joe."

"Yes, Mr. Z.?"

"Sleep in tomorrow morning. You'll need your rest if you're going to start courting Gretchen."

"No, I'll be to work at the regular time, but thanks anyway." And he was gone.

Dallas closed the door and turned to Shay and, without saying a word, pulled her into his arms. "Now you've made two people happy."

"Isn't it fun to help people? He was on top of the world. I'll bet Gretchen isn't sleeping, but I'll bet she's dreaming."

"Shay, you act more like a Christian than most Christians. Too bad you're going to miss heaven."

"What?"

"You can live a good life and do all kinds of good things, but unless you accept Jesus into your heart, you're not going to heaven. You should give that some thought." He kissed her on the top of the head and let her go. "We'd better get to bed. I can't sleep in tomorrow morning either."

"Dallas, you can't drop this heaven thing on me and then expect me to go to sleep."

"I'm sorry, but I can't make the decision for you. You have to do that."

He took her hand and led her up the steps to her room. "Good night, dear." He went on down the hall to his room.

Shay stood there and watched him go. She was mad. Why did he say she was going to hell? Well, I guess that wasn't what he said, but if she wasn't going to heaven, hell was where she was going. She had been thinking about it, but she just wasn't ready yet to get into this religion thing. Why couldn't they just be friends, but she knew his religion, or walking with Jesus as he liked to put it, was real important to him.

She fell asleep the minute her head hit the pillow, and she dreamed of heaven. It was just like a preacher on television had explained it. She didn't believe it at the time, but now it was so real. She started running toward the city, but the faster she ran, the farther away it seemed. She could never quite get there. She awoke with a start and looked at the clock. She had only been sleeping for twelve minutes and could not go back to sleep again for a long time.

CHAPTER FIFTEEN

Martha was standing at the kitchen sink, washing the last of the breakfast dishes. It wouldn't be long, and she would have to start dinner for the guys who were branding cattle at the southeast corrals. This was the third day they had worked there, and they should finish with that bunch of cattle before the day was up. Then they would move up to the northwest section of the ranch and do those cattle. That would leave only two smaller groups, which shouldn't take more than a day, maybe two, to complete. She didn't know why the men expected such a big feed at branding time, but it was the tradition, and she wasn't about to break it. Maria, Pedro's wife, who usually helped her, was home sick again today, and so Martha was here all by herself. Maria had been sick the last several mornings, and Martha had a suspicion it wasn't the flu. There would probably be a little one coming along in the next few months. It was a beautiful day, and as she looked out across the Missouri River, she thanked God for his wonderful creation. She was worried about Dallas and the load he had to carry since his folks' death. With the cattle price's down, the pasture about gone because of the lack of rain, then the fire took over half of what pasture they had plus most of their hay, she knew he had a lot on his mind. She knew he had a big loan, which had to be paid. It was a big load for a young man. "Please, God, lay your hand on him and guide him in your ways. Help him to make the right decisions. I love you and thank you for all you've done for Hank and me. We pray, Lord—" There was a knock on the door.

"Hello, is anybody home?" a cheerful voice called out.

"In here, Shay," Martha answered.

As Shay walked into the kitchen and hung her jacket on one of the pegs, Martha said, "Oh, am I glad to see you. I'm going to put you to work."

"That's what I'm here for. I knew that they were branding, and I thought I might be able to do something to help. I'm sorry I didn't get here sooner."

"I am glad you're here. You sure can help. Maria is sick today, so I'm kind of shorthanded."

"Oh, what's wrong with her? That's Pedro's wife, isn't it?"

"Yes, it is. I think it may be morning sickness. I don't think it is the flu."

"Oh, wouldn't that be great? What can I do?"

"I just finished up the breakfast dishes and was about to start dinner. I think there are fifteen or twenty guys out there, and I know they'll be hungry as a bunch of grizzly bears by dinner. First, I'm going to sit down and have a cup of coffee and rest for a spell. I'm not as young as I used to be, and I'm not near as fast."

"You sit down," said Shay. "Let me get the coffee for you."

"Please join me."

"I will."

In a few minutes, they were sitting at one end of the big plank table with the log legs. Sometimes, there were one or two people for a meal at this table, and sometimes, the table was full. You never knew from one day to the next which meal would be busy and which meal would be slow. This was just how it was on the ranch. As Shay warmed her hands over the cup of coffee, she looked across the table at Martha. She was a beautiful woman with just a slight streak of gray in her dark brown hair, which was always well kept. Shay guessed her to be in her early sixties although she didn't look near that old. She was just a wonderful person.

"What?" Martha asked.

"I didn't say anything," answered Shay.

"I know, but you have a question in your eyes."

"A girl doesn't have a chance with you," answered Shay. "Okay, I'll tell you why I came. I did come to help, but mostly I wanted to talk to you.

"Okay, here it goes. As you know, Dallas is very religious, and he's been trying to explain it to me, but I'm pretty dumb. To tell you the truth, I wasn't real interested at first. But then being around him and you and

Hank and some of the other ranch hands, I'm changing my mind. You're all so happy, and even though Dallas is under a lot of pressure, he isn't all stressed out about it. I don't know much about it, and I don't know the Bible at all. Dallas said the most important verse in the whole book is John 3:16. Well, I read it and read it. In fact, I've read it so many times that I've memorized it, but I'm not sure I understand it."

"Well, let's take a look," said Martha and at the same time saying under her breath, "Lord, help me to say the right thing to guide Shay into your kingdom." She reached behind her and took a Bible off the shelf. "Let's see what it says."

"For God loved the world so much," Shay quoted, "that he gave his only son so that anyone who believes in him shall not perish but have eternal life."

"Very good," said Martha, "let's just break it down."

"'For God,' do you believe in God and that the Bible is his word?"

"Yes."

"Okay, so we've established there is a god, right?"

"Yes."

"'Loved the world,' that's pretty broad. Let's make it more personal."

"For God loved Shay Everheart. You're part of the world, right?"

"Yes, I guess so." She grinned.

"'That he gave,' what did he give? His only beloved, the only son he had, the most valuable thing he had, he gave it for you.

"What did that Son of God do? He died on the cross for you. For who?"

"The world."

"And who is the world?"

"Me."

"For God loved Shay Everhart so much that he gave his son who died on the cross, for your sins and mine."

"'That anyone,' meaning Shay Everhart, believes on him. What do you get for believing on him?" Martha asked?

"I don't get punished and I have eternal life. But don't I have to do something?"

"Sure, if you wanted a cookie to go with that coffee, what would you do?"

"I guess I would ask you for one."

"That's what you do if you want to accept the forgiveness that Jesus died for. Do you think you're a sinner and need his forgiveness?"

"Yes, I do. I really do."
"Just repeat after me.
"Dear Jesus."
"Dear Jesus," Shay said as she started to cry.
"I am a sinner."
"I am a sinner."
"I believe your son Jesus died for my sins."
"I believe your son Jesus died for my sins."
"And I want you to forgive me."
"And I want you to forgive me."
"Thank you, Amen."
"Thank you, Amen."
"Is that all there is to it?"
"That's all," said Martha as she turned to I John 1:9. "Here read this."

Shay read, "'But if we confess our sins to him, he can be depended on to forgive us and to cleanse us from every wrong.'"

"What does it say?" asked Martha.

"If I confess my sins, he will forgive me."

"Did you confess?"

"Yes, so I'm forgiven." A big smile came across Shay's face. "I feel so clean. The weight is gone." Martha came around the table and threw her arms around Shay. They stood and cried together.

Some time later, Martha looked at the clock. "Oh my, we better get going, or all the men are going to be mad at us." By eleven-thirty, they had enough food packed in the van to feed an army. There was fried chicken, meat loaf, potatoes and gravy, baked beans, corn, a macaroni hot dish, along with three kinds of bread, cake, pie, and cookies.

"How many men are out there anyway?" Shay asked.

"Oh, fifteen or twenty."

"Are they going to eat all this food?"

"Oh yes, they've been working hard since breakfast at five thirty this morning without anything to eat but coffee and some caramel rolls I sent along. About sundown, they'll be looking for more."

"Did you do that all by yourself?"

"Yep, just me and the Lord."

"Why in the world didn't you call me? I could have come out earlier."

"Dallas told me to, but I didn't want to impose on you."

"Don't ever do that again, Martha. I'm more than happy to come and help."

"Well, I think we have everything. Let's get going. It's about ten miles down to where they're branding."

Some of the guys were just finishing up the morning work, and the rest were standing around the tables they had hauled down that morning, waiting for the banquet to arrive. When Martha and Shay pulled in with the van, a cheer went up from the men.

Dallas was talking to a couple of the cowboys, and when he saw Shay get out of the van, he said, "I see you finally took my advice and called her."

"No, I didn't call. She just came on her own."

"Thank you, Shay, I appreciate that."

They put all of the food on one table, but before the guys started dishing up what they wanted, Dallas took off his hat and said, "Let's ask the Lord to bless the food." In his deep voice, he thanked the Lord for what they had accomplished that morning and for the protection while they were taking care of his cattle. He thanked him for the food and asked the Lord to bless Martha and Shay for preparing it. Then the guys dove in, almost before he said amen. Shay watched in total amazement as they filled their plates and then came back for seconds and sometimes thirds.

Dallas came over to where Shay was standing and said, "Thanks for coming out and helping Martha. I was worried about her when I heard Maria was sick."

"You should have called me."

"I told Martha to call you."

"I said you should have called me, not Martha, but I'm glad I'm here. I wouldn't have missed it for anything. This morning was the best morning of my life."

"Do you enjoy cooking that much?"

"No, Dallas, this morning I asked Jesus to come into my heart."

"You what!" he said in total disbelief.

"You heard me."

Dallas threw his arms around her, lifting her off the ground. He spun around several times. "I'm so happy for you," he whispered as he was doing it. When he set her down, he kissed the top of her head. She looked up at him with tears in her eyes. Dallas still had his arms around Shay when he hollered, "Guys!" Suddenly it was quiet and all eyes were on them. "Shay has something to tell you." He looked down at her.

"What?" she asked.

"Tell them what you just told me."

"Now?"

"Yes."

She cleared her throat and, with bold confidence, said, "This morning, sitting at the kitchen table in the ranch house, Martha helped me to ask Jesus to come into my heart. From this day on, I'm going to live for him." A roar went up from the men, hats flew in the air, and everybody applauded. Before she knew it, the cowboys were crowded around her, shaking her hand, patting her on the back, and hugging her. She looked at Dallas, who stood a way off. He had a big grin on his face while tears ran down his cheeks.

"Well that calls for another piece of pie," said Pedro as he headed for the table again. How the guys could go back to work after eating the way they did, Shay didn't know, but shortly after dinner, some climbed into the saddle and went looking for more cows and calves, and the rest started branding and giving shots. Martha and Shay loaded what was left into the van.

Just before they pulled out, Dallas came over and said, "You're staying for supper, aren't you?"

"Sure am, Martha needs the help."

"I don't suppose I could hire you to help Martha until we're done with the branding?"

"You haven't got enough money to get me to stay and cook for this bunch of vultures. I can't believe the amount of food they can devour. But I'll gladly do it for nothing."

"Thanks, Shay, I owe you one."

"You owe me more than one, boy," she said, punching him in the gut and climbing into the driver's seat of the van.

As Martha and Shay retraced the trail or gravel road or whatever it was across the rolling hills of the ranch, Shay was once again taken in by the beauty of the West River country. She was again reminded of a quote by Louis Toothman, "To view the mountains you only need your eyes, but to view the prairie requires the soul," or something like that. Shay swerved to miss a big snake sunning himself in the middle of the road.

"Wow! Did you see that," she said to Martha.

"Yeah, there are a few rattlers in this part of the country, and they like to sun themselves in the warm sand."

"I didn't know there were rattlesnakes in South Dakota?"

"Oh, sure you see them quite often."

Shay didn't say anything for a while as they bumped along the gravel road. She was enjoying the time she got to spend on the Z bar 3.

"Why were the men so excited when I told them I had asked Jesus to come into my heart?"

"Well, you see, all of the men that are working out there are Christians, and they're just happy to see a new soul born into the family of God. They know how important it is to have Christ in your life for encouragement and someone to go to in time of trouble. Most of these guys are going through a real hard time with the cattle prices down and no rain. A lot of them have to buy hay and feed. If it weren't for their strong faith in God, they just wouldn't make it."

"Does it really make that much difference? Is that why Dallas is so happy even though he's under so much pressure?"

"Yes, it is. Most men his age couldn't run a ranch this big, even when times were good. If it wasn't for the big loan his dad left him, he wouldn't be in trouble, but now the way things are, he may even lose the ranch. No matter what happens, Dallas will still trust God.

"Shay, you've been good for Dallas. He's happier whenever you're around. His eyes sparkle again like they use to shine whenever your name is even mentioned."

"I hope so. I enjoy being around him. In fact, this whole ranch thing is starting to grow on me."

By the time they got back to the ranch and had things put away, it was almost time to start supper. It was a lot of work cooking for that many men, but Shay enjoyed it. She really liked being with Martha. They had everything ready to go by the time the first pickup arrived, and they threw a bunch of steaks on the grill. Before the guys even had time to wash up, the steaks were cooked to perfection, and they started to eat. Shay didn't put the next batch of steaks on until she saw the next truckload arrive. That way, they were hot off the grill, cooked like each man ordered it. When the third group was ready to eat, the first ones were finished and off to the bunkhouse to shower and hit the hay. Five-thirty in the morning came pretty early. Dallas was one of the last to eat, and by the time he was done, Shay was at the sink washing dishes. He picked up a dish towel and started drying plates.

"You don't have to do that. I'll get it. Go take a shower and put your pajamas on. You need your rest."

"I don't wear pajamas, and besides, I'm not tired. I will go take a shower though. Can I talk to you later?"

"Am I going to get fired?"

"Slaves can't be fired. They have to be sold."

"Then I'm safe! Nobody would pay anything for me."

"Oh, you might be surprised."

Dallas finished drying the plates and laid down the towel. "I'll be back," he said.

Shay sent Martha to bed. "You need to get off your feet," she said.

She was just finishing up a few things around the kitchen when Dallas walked in.

"This ranch life is a little tough on a city girl, right?"

"Oh, I'm doing all right. I think I am starting to like it."

"How can you? We work you so hard. What about your job in the big city?"

"Oh, I got fired from that."

"I'm not surprised, all the time you spend out here."

"No, it's because I asked too many questions about out here."

"Want a cup of coffee? I made a fresh pot. I thought some of the guys might want a snack before they went to bed."

"No wonder they all like you. You're such a sweetheart."

"What did you call me?"

"A sweetheart."

"Why, thank you. Here let me pour that for you. You better have a couple of cookies to go with the coffee."

"Come on, let's sit in the den. It's more comfortable in there."

"Okay."

They walked into the cozy dimly lit den and sat down in chairs facing each other.

"Now, what did you want to talk to me about? Did I do something wrong?" asked Shay.

"No, I just wanted to get you alone. I didn't want to share you with anybody else. It was kind of a crazy day."

"This was a great day. It was so much fun working with Martha."

"What made you decide to turn your life over to Christ?"

"You."

"Me? I didn't preach at you, did I?"

"No, not in words but your way of life was different. You were happy in spite of all the stress and pressure you are under. You have peace and joy. I didn't have that, and I wondered why. Remember you told me to read John 3:16? I did, over and over again. In fact I read it so many times that I memorized it. I thought I knew what it meant, but I wasn't sure, so I asked Martha. She explained it to me, and I was pretty much right, but it seemed so simple when she explained it. I thought there must be something that I had to do, but she said all I had to do was ask. It was a free gift, and so I did. I asked, and Jesus came into my heart."

"What happened?"

"I felt a weight lift off me. I really can't explain it, but I was different. When you told me to tell the guys. At first, I was scared, and then I just wanted to tell the whole world what had happened to me. I'm really not a very brave person, but somehow I had power and confidence."

"That's what Christ does for you and that's why I wanted you to tell the guys because it makes you so much stronger. I knew what the guys would do. I knew they would be so happy for you. I didn't like them hugging you, but I guess in this case, it was okay."

"Oh, don't be silly." she said, laughing. "You've never given me a hug like that."

"I didn't know you wanted one."

They talked far into the night, much later then they should have. Finally Shay said, "We have to go to bed. You have a lot of work to do tomorrow, and I have to start breakfast pretty soon. Here, let me take your cup." She reached out to take it, but he grabbed her hand and pulled her onto his lap.

"I think I will put you on the payroll so you have to do whatever I want."

"It seems to me that's what I'm doing now!" They both laughed.

Shay put her arms around his neck and gave him a big hug and kissed him on the forehead. "Good night, Dallas." She got up and took the cups back into the kitchen.

She sensed him behind her. "I'm sorry, Shay. I didn't mean to take advantage of you."

"You didn't. I was hoping you did it on purpose!" She smiled at him. "Now go to bed," she said, putting her hand on his arm.

"I'll see you in the morning, Shay." He started up the stairs to the second floor and his room.

"Dallas." He stopped, and Shay slowly walked up the stairs to where he had stopped. When she got to where he was standing, she put both her arms gently around his neck, pulled him toward her, and gave him a kiss that he would not soon forget. "Good night, dear." She pulled away and walked to her room. Before she closed the door, she looked back, and he was staring after her with a dazed look on his face.

"Do you expect me to go to sleep now>" he asked before she closed the door.

As Shay got ready for bed, she thought to herself, *What is this guy doing to me? I can't even think straight.*

Little did she realize that Dallas was thinking the same thing about her!

CHAPTER SIXTEEN

It seemed like she had just gotten to sleep when the alarm went off. She rolled over and looked at the clock. It was 4:30 a.m. and still dark outside. She wanted to lie back down on the pillow and snuggle under the warm comforter, but she knew that if she did, it would be a long time before she woke up again. Sitting up on the edge of the bed, she stretched and yawned and finally stumbled into the bathroom. After splashing some cold water on her face and running a brush through her hair, she started to feel more alive. She was glad she had set the alarm because she would never have gotten up, and she knew that Martha needed the help getting breakfast for the bunch of men.

She slipped into her jeans, boots, and a white lacy Western blouse that was tight enough to show that she was a woman but comfortable to work in. With just a touch of makeup and some nice earrings, she stepped out into the hall or balcony. Dallas's door was still closed, and she wondered if he would be able to get up this morning after she kept him up so late last night. She really should have sent him to bed earlier, but she so much enjoyed the time they could be together. Tiptoeing down the steps so as to wake no one, she made her way to the kitchen to get the coffee on and start breakfast. As she rounded the corner, she saw there was already a light on, and she could smell the coffee brewing.

Martha was standing in front of the refrigerator, taking out some things she needed, when Shay said, "Good morning, what can I do to help?"

Martha jumped, "Oh, you startled me. I didn't know you were up. You sure didn't have to get up this morning. I don't want to work you to death."

"I was afraid I would get fired if I didn't get up. You know how mean the boss is. Besides, where would I find another job as good as this one?"

"I am not mean," said Dallas. Shay whirled around, and there he sat at the end of the long table with a cup of coffee in one hand and his Bible in the other.

"What are you doing up already?" Shay asked.

"I work here, and you know how mean the boss is."

Shay walked over and messed up his hair. "He really isn't as mean as he tries to make people think he is. Really, he's just a big teddy bear." She gave him a little hug. "What should I do?" she asked Martha.

"Why don't you slice some of those leftover baked potatoes we had last night, and I'll get the bacon and ham frying. We won't fry the eggs until the guys start coming in. We'll wait to start the toast then too."

It wasn't long before Hank and Joe came in, and Martha said, "Let's feed these three guys and get them out of the way before the rest get here."

"Rusty and Pedro will be here in a minute. They were just ready to leave the bunkhouse when I did," Joe said.

Shay started putting the food on the table, and Martha fried eggs and buttered toast faster than any short-order cook Shay had ever seen. By five thirty all of the men had been fed and were on their way out the door and onto the work of the day. As Dallas went past Shay on his way out with the other men, he said, "Maybe tonight we can sit down and go over the first two chapters of John. Did you have a chance to read them?"

"I sure did, and I have some questions written down."

"Good, this should be a lot of fun. Tell Martha to not work you so hard so you can stay awake." He patted her cheek as he left.

"What are you suppose to tell me?" asked Martha as she walked back into the kitchen.

"Oh, Dallas and I are going to look at the first two chapters of John tonight, and he said to tell you not to work me too hard so I could stay awake."

"That's so good. Get into the Word and study it with someone else. It will be good for Dallas to have to really think to answer any questions you might have, and it will be good for you to learn from someone as knowledgeable as Dallas."

"I'm looking forward to it."

"The more you study God's Word, the better Christian you will become."

That noon when Martha and Shay brought out lunch to where the guys were working, she noticed that Dallas wasn't there. She asked Hank where he was and found out that Dallas and Rusty had ridden farther north to see if there were any cattle up there. Hank was pretty sure there was some missing. Before the men finished eating, Shay saw Dallas and Rusty come over one of the hills about half a mile in the distance, and she started getting their plates ready so they could eat as soon as they got there. As they rode into camp, Dallas said to Hank, "You were right. There were some cows missing. We found six of them up by the water hole in the northeast quarter."

"Why didn't you bring them back with you?"

"They were dead."

"Dead?"

"Yep, and I don't know why. It looks like they just lay down and died."

"Better get the vet out to take a look at them, probably the sheriff too, the way things have been going around here."

"Yes, I think you're right. Hank, why don't you go back with the girls and call those guys?"

"Okay, I'd rather go with the girls than stay here anyway."

Within about three hours, both the vet and the sheriff were at the ranch, and Hank took them up to where the cattle were. Dallas and the crew were finished with the branding and were back to the ranch before Hank and the lawman were back. Dallas was sitting in the kitchen, having a cup of coffee and talking to Martha and Shay when he saw them ride in. He shoved his chair back and said, "I guess I'll go out and see what they think about the situation."

"Can I come with you?" asked Shay.

"Sure."

As they walked out on the porch, the guys were just climbing down off their horses, and they turned them over to a couple of the cowboys who had come out to help them. They started for the house, and Dallas and Shay walked out to meet them.

"Well, boys, what do you think?" asked Dallas.

"I think," said the sheriff, "that this is a clean one. I think it was just a freak accident, don't you, Ralph?"

"Yes," said the vet, "my first guess is they died from blue-green algae. Under the right conditions and temperature, these watering holes can produce enough poison to kill a cow. It doesn't happen very often, but that's what I think it is. I took some tissue samples and will send them in just to make sure."

"I looked around real good and couldn't find any signs of foul play," said the sheriff. "I know with all the things that have been going on around here, the first thing you think of is somebody killed them, but I don't think that's the case this time."

"I guess I'm glad to hear that," said Dallas, "not that I like losing the cattle, but at least it wasn't somebody out to get us. Thanks for all your time, fellows."

"I'll let you know if I find out anything different," said the vet as he and the sheriff walked back to their pickups.

Shay looked up at Dallas with sadness in her eyes. "If it isn't one thing, it's another."

"Yes, darling, but all things work together for good to them who love God."

"Darling? I like that. I hope some day I can have faith like you do."

"You will. In fact, you make my faith stronger."

"I do? How?"

"Well, sometimes, I say I know things will work out because I know it's the right thing to say, but you, if you see something in God's Word, you just believe it because he said it. That's the way it should be. You have faith like a little child and sometimes mine is so mature it doesn't work as good anymore. Does that make sense?"

"Yes, I think so. What you're saying is it isn't all that difficult. If God says it, believe it."

"See what I mean? You bring me back to the basics."

"Hey, kids, supper is ready," Martha called from the back porch.

"Oh, I should have been helping," said Shay as she turned and ran up the steps.

"I'm sorry, Martha. I should have been in here helping you instead of sticking my nose into Dallas's ranch business."

"No, you shouldn't have. I've worked you way too hard the way it was, and with the army gone and the cowboys back on there own and it's just the four of us, this is a breeze. I didn't have time to put on a skirt for dinner, but I guess Hank will forgive me this time."

"Do you always put on a skirt for meals?"

"No, just dinner or supper or whatever you call it. Some women think that a way to a man's heart is through his stomach, but it's really through his eyes. It gets me a lot of points to look nice for Hank."

"You are so wise," said Shay. "Let's do it. They're still talking out on the porch."

They were back in the kitchen, putting the last of the supper on the table when the men came in.

"You look nice tonight, dear," said Hank.

Dallas didn't say anything but looked at Shay from her high heels to her fresh makeup. A smile spread across his face, and he reached out and squeezed her hand. She knew he liked what he saw. It was good to be back to almost normal, and not have to cook for an army. It was nice to just sit down and have a quiet meal with just the four of them. It was starting to seem like she belonged here. Little did she know that Dallas was feeling the same way. It was also amazing to Shay how Martha could come up with such a delicious meal out of the leftovers from lunch. Shay had already learned so much from her, and she was looking forward to learning a lot more.

Dallas and Hank spent most of the time while they were eating talking about the cattle that were found dead that afternoon, and Shay and Martha talked about all the food they had prepared for the cowboys. They had finished their meal and were just sitting there, drinking the last cup of coffee when Shay kicked off her high heel and ran the toe of her nylon foot up under Dallas's pant leg. She felt him look at her, but she was looking off in the distance, acting like nothing was going on. Finally, as she rubbed his leg, she looked at him and smiled. He winked back at her, and she took her foot away and slipped her shoe back on. Shay got up and started picking up the dishes. "Here," she said to Martha, "have another cup of coffee, and I'll clean this mess up."

"No, I'll help you."

"Hank," Shay said, "make your wife relax. She's been working too hard the last few days."

"Darling," he said, "listen to Shay. You'll hurt her feelings if you don't."

In just a few minutes, Shay had the dishes in the dishwasher and came back and sat down at the table.

"Thanks, Shay, it's been a long time since I just sat here and watched somebody else do the dishes. I think I'll keep you around." She patted Shay's arm.

"Well, don't you two stay up all night," Hank said. We have work to do in the morning. Come on, Ma. Let's give these two young ones a little space." He reached out his hand to Martha. After they had left the room,

Dallas said, "Let's go sit in front of the fireplace and get started on this Bible study."

"Let me run up to my room and get my Bible you gave me."

"You don't have to do that. There's one right here."

"No, I want to get my own. I have some questions written down. Besides, I want to take some notes, and I want them in my own Bible." When Shay came back down, Dallas was sitting in front of the fireplace. He had kicked off his boots and had his feet up on the coffee table.

"Does your mother, I mean, Martha let you do that?"

"Martha is just like my mother, only better. She lets me get by with murder."

"Yes, I've noticed you're pretty spoiled."

Shay sat down on the couch, and Dallas said, "Slide over by me so I can look at your Bible. That way, I don't have to walk clear upstairs and get mine.

"Let's pray." He took both of Shay's hands in his. "Dear Lord, we thank you for this day and for your guidance and protection. Now as Shay and I look into your Word, open our eyes so that we can see just what you have in there for us. Amen."

Shay looked up into Dallas's face while holding on to his hands. "You're a very special friend."

"Thank you, that means a lot to me," Dallas answered.

"Okay," said Shay, "I've read the lesson assigned to me and have written down some questions."

"Fine, but let's just read through the first chapter and talk about it as we go along."

"Whatever you say, teacher." Shay grinned at Dallas.

"Remember I gave you a Living Bible because it was easier to understand?" Dallas opened it to the first chapter of John and started reading. "'Before anything else existed, there was Christ with God. He has always been alive and is himself God.' John kind of starts in the middle of Jesus's life, but these first couple of verses is telling us that Jesus is God and always was. Now if you want the first few years of Jesus's life here on Earth, you can read that in either Matthew or Luke. These two books start out with the birth of Jesus. John starts out with his ministry, which started when he was about thirty years old." Dallas read on, and when he stopped he said, "Here we find the man who came before Jesus to announce his coming. John the Baptist was actually a cousin of Jesus, but he was not the first one to tell of his coming. See here in verse 45, Moses, way back in the Old Testament, talked about Jesus's coming. In fact a lot of the Old Testament is prophecy of his coming. Right after Jesus is baptized by John, he starts his ministry and begins to find his disciples. These are the ones that will be with him throughout his time here on earth, the ones he will teach to carry on his work after he's gone."

"It sounds so easy to understand when you read it. I read it several times, and it wasn't as clear as you reading it one time."

"Well, remember, Shay, most of these stories were told to me by my mother long before I was old enough to read, and I've read them several times since. That's why I wanted to discuss them with you and help you understand them. The more you read, the easier it will be. Actually the Bible and its stories are pretty simple and easy to understand if we just take what the Word says. I know that there are a lot of theologians who do deep studies of the Bible, but I think that God meant it to be simple so that even a child could understand it."

"I like this," said Shay. "Read chapter 2."

Dallas started reading chapter 2, adding his thoughts to the story as he went along. From time to time, Shay stopped him with a question, and he would explain it, and they would take as much time as was needed for Shay to understand. It was late again, way too late when they finally finished and climbed the stairs to bed.

CHAPTER SEVENTEEN

Ever since Shay went to the Z bar 3, she had not been satisfied with her condo. It just didn't have any warmth or beauty like the house on the ranch. She thought about remodeling it, but then maybe it would be easier just to find a different one, one that was more like what she had in mind and wouldn't take so much to do over. One evening, she got on the Internet and looked at real estate in the Rapid City area that was for sale. There was a couple that caught her eye, so the next day she went to the real estate company that had the listing.

"Can we help you?" asked the receptionist as she walked into the office of Remax.

"Yes, last night I was on the Internet and saw a couple of places I would like to take a look at."

"Did you by any chance get the numbers of the units?"

"Yes, I did," she said, handing the girl the numbers.

"Good, that make's it much easier. I'll get Mary Axelrod to show you." After the introductions and some small talk, Shay followed Mary to the first place. She looked at the first two, and although they were nice on the outside, they weren't much different than her own condo on the inside. They both would take a lot of work to make them into the type of living she had in mind. The third one was a little better but still wasn't what she was looking for. Maybe she would never find anything that she liked as much as the ranch house on the Z bar 3. She never thought a city girl like her would ever long for the quiet beauty of the West River country. Oh, she was from the big wide open state of Texas but had lived her whole life in Houston. She thanked Mary Axelrod for her time and was just getting into her car when another car pulled up with two men in it. Who should get out of the passengers side but Barry Killmee?

"Hi, Shay, I haven't seen you around for a while. Are you house shopping?"

"Yes, just doing some looking."

"Find anything that you like?"

"No, not really."

"Just what do you have in mind?"

"Oh, I'm looking for something kind of rustic, with a Western flavor."

"Man, I have just the thing. I'm sure you would really like it, listed it just this morning. Want to take a look at it?"

"No, I wouldn't buy anything from Jippem."

"Don't worry about that. I can run it through a friend of mine." Shay was really hesitant about going anywhere with Barry, but at the same time if she had a chance to talk to him, maybe she could find out why they were so interested in the Z bar 3.

"Sure, why not?" she said.

"Oh," he said, "I don't have a car. I rode out here with this other agent. We were just going to look this place over. Would you mind driving and then drop me off at the office?"

"No, I guess you can go with me."

Barry went in the house to tell his partner what he was going to do while Shay waited outside. "Hey, Jim, I'm going with Shay. You just go back to the office when you're through. You can fill me in on this place in the morning. I'm going to show her another place."

"Well, don't try to get her in bed. You know she almost killed the old man when he tried."

"You know I won't do that unless I have a chance." Barry grinned.

They went out and looked at the place, but it wasn't at all what she had in mind. On the way back to the office where Barry's car was parked, he said, "How about letting me buy you dinner?"

"No, I don't think so. You're married, remember? You better go home to your wife."

"Oh, she isn't even home, and besides, we're getting a divorce."

"Sure, I've heard that one before."

"No, really."

Before she was a Christian, it wouldn't have made any difference, but now she knew it wasn't right. But she still wondered if he knew something about the Z bar 3 and could she get some information from him. That would be the only reason she would even consider going to dinner with a slime ball like him.

"Okay," she said, "I am pretty hungry." They stopped at a steak house that Shay had been to before. The food was always good there. The host led them to a booth by the window, and Shay sat with her back to the door.

The waitress laid down the menus and asked, "Can I get you something to drink?"

"Yes, I'll have a scotch," said Barry.

"And you, miss?"

"Coke."

"No, no," said Barry, "the lady will have a martini."

"No, I'll have a Coke. I don't drink anymore."

"Oh, have just one." He was hoping to get her liquored up to help a little later that evening.

"No, Coke," she insisted, and the host left the table.

"You're no fun."

"This isn't supposed to be fun. This is just dinner."

"You know I'm getting a divorce, don't you?"

"Yes, you told me that."

Before the steaks came, Barry had already had two more drinks and was getting pretty mouthy. By the time they had finished eating, he was trying to impress her as to how big the deals were he was swinging in the office. "You know, Shay, I'm kind of glad you quit Jippem. He thought you could go out and sleep with the guy a time or two and come back with a signed contract. Well, it just doesn't work that way. I've met with that Ziglar guy, and he's nothing but a goody-two-shoes. I'll bet he's never even been with a woman. He probably wouldn't know what to do if he did have one."

"Are you going to get the job done?" asked Shay

"Yep, I'll get it done. I'm good at that kind of thing."

"How are you going to do it?"

"Money, lots of money. Money will get you anything."

"When I was out there, it didn't seem like he wanted to sell no matter what the price was."

"Oh, I know that. You just have to know how to work it. I've worked these tough cases before."

"I know you're one of the top salesmen at Jippem," Shay said to egg him on.

"Yeah, I make more money than all the other guys put together. You just have to know how to work these big ones."

"How will you go about it?" asked Shay.

"Well," he motioned to the waitress, "you know he has a big mortgage on the ranch?"

"Yes, sir?" said the waitress as she walked up.

"Bring me another drink. Do you want anything else, Shay?"

"No, I'm fine."

"And I don't think he can come up with the money," he continued. "Just to make it a little worse, some of his cattle were shot, and they also had a fire, so he has to buy hay."

"Were some of his cattle shot?" asked Shay.

"Yes, that's what I hear."

"Do they know who did it?"

"No, but I know a guy who knows a guy who does those kind of things. That dumb sheriff out there will never figure it out in a million years."

"How do you arrange something like that?"

"You just have to know the right people," bragged Barry.

"But the fire, that was probably started by lighting or something," Shay said.

"Yeah right, I said you just have to have the right people."

"Bring me another drink," Barry said to a waitress as she walked by.

"Why is Jippem so intent on buying that ranch? There are so many other ranches for sale."

"Jippem has had his eye on that ranch for a long time but never had the money to swing the deal. Its location right on the Missouri River is going to make it a great development. He's planning on building a lodge and a golf course. The tarred airstrip that's already there will make it easy for the rich people from the city who want to play cowboy to get their jets in. The log cabins he's going to build will be sold on time share. He's been dreaming and planning this for a long time and now he has the cash to do it."

"Where did he get the financing to do all this?"

"Financing nothing. He's dealing only in cash."

"How's he going to swing that?"

"Waitress, bring me another drink."

By this time, Barry was really getting drunk, and the words flowed almost as freely as the drinks. He thought he was really impressing Shay, which should make her want him later on that night. Barry forgot Shay's last question, so she asked it again. "Where is Jippem going to get the cash to do all this?"

"I shouldn't be telling you this, but I know you can keep a secret. He met this guy from California who has a lot of cash that he has to get back in the system. This is a way he can do it. You see, if he gives the cash to Jippem who buys land and builds building and then Jippem sells the time shares, he has the money back, and it's clean."

"Where did this guy get all the cash?"

"Well, I can't say that, but you know there are things going on in the United States that aren't above board. I think you know what I mean."

"You mean drugs?"

"You said it. I didn't," said Barry. Shay dropped the subject when Barry asked if she would like some ice cream.

"Sure, that sounds good."

"I told Jippem I wanted in for at least ten percent above my commission. When I get that baby, maybe you and I can take off for South America and live like kings."

"What about your wife?"

"Didn't I tell you we're getting a divorce? Besides I would rather spend the money with you."

Shay decided she would try one more question. "Have you met the man with all the cash, or is Jippem keeping that from you?"

"No, I'm in on the whole deal," Barry bragged. "His name is Ben Shark from San Diego, California. I talk to him all the time."

"I'm really proud of you, the way you can handle the big ones," said Shay as she picked up her purse. "Excuse me for a minute, I need to go to the little girl's room."

"Sure, I'm going to have one more drink, and then we'll blow this place and maybe go to a motel. What do you say?" But Shay was out of earshot, around the corner, and out the front door. She ran to her car and tore out of the parking lot.

* * *

It was about two o'clock in the afternoon when Dallas came down the stairs into the kitchen. Martha was just taking two loaves of bread out of the oven when he walked in.

"Don't plan on me being here for supper," he said. "I'm going into Rapid City and surprise Shay and take her out for dinner. I haven't seen her for over a week, and it's not the same when she's not here."

"She's a mighty fine woman, Dallas. Whenever you ask her to marry you, you have my blessing."

"Why, thank you, Martha. That means a lot to me. I guess I look at you as my mother since Mom died." He gave her a hug.

"You need a mother to keep you going in the right direction. I remember that one girl . . ."

"That's enough of that. I learned my lesson that time."

Dallas put a bag in the backseat of his truck just in case he decided to stay overnight. It was a long way into Rapid and almost as far back. He had washed his truck that morning, but by the time he got to the interstate, it was hard to tell. They hadn't had any rain for so long that the pickup was covered with dust from the gravel roads. He still had a lot of miles from where he hit the interstate into Rapid City, and it was getting late. He hoped that Shay hadn't already eaten. He should have called first, but that would have taken the surprise out of the whole evening. As he took the exit ramp on the east edge of town, on the way to her condo, he stopped for the stop sign. Off to his right was the Wagon Wheel Steak House, and there was Shay's car in the parking lot. He was sure of it. He pulled into the parking lot and drove up to her car. That was definitely her car as he looked at the personalized license plate—"SHAY."

He parked his truck and was walking up to the door when he looked through the window. There sat Shay with another guy. He stopped in his tracks as his heart hit the sidewalk. She had her back to the window and didn't see him. He turned around and half ran and half walked back to his truck. So much for the surprise. He was the one who got the surprise. As he drove back to the Z bar 3, he talked to himself, he talked to God, and then he talked to himself again. He had trusted her. He thought they had something more than just friendship. How could he have been so mistaken? When she kissed him, was she just putting on an act? What was all the talk about liking the ranch and the West River country? Was she just playing with him? He didn't think so, but now she was with another guy. Is this why she always had to go back to town? Had this been going on for a long time? All he had was questions, no answers.

When he got back to the ranch, Martha and Hank were still up watching TV. He didn't realize they were still up until he walked in the front door, and there they sat. He didn't want to talk to them or anybody else. He just wanted to crawl in a hole and pull the dirt in after him. This wasn't the end of his life, but it might just as well have been.

"Couldn't you find Shay?" asked Hank as he walked in.

"Oh, I found her all right," said Dallas as he started up the stairs. "She was out with another guy."

"What?" asked Martha with surprise.

"You heard me."

"Did you talk to her?"

"I didn't have to. I'm not blind."

"Well, maybe it was her brother."

"She doesn't have a brother."

"Listen, Dallas," she said with such force that he turned around at the top of the stairs. "There is an explanation for this. Shay is not the kind of girl who would play with your heart."

"Whatever you say. You're always right," he said as he walked down the hall to his room. He threw himself on the bed and cried. He tried to pray and he tried to sleep. Neither came easy.

* * *

Barry finished his latest drink and wondered why it was taking Shay so long. How long she had been gone, he really didn't know. He had had so many drinks by this time he had lost track of time, but what difference did it make? He was going to do his best to stretch this dinner into the rest of the night in some motel somewhere. He looked up through his bleary eyes just as Jippem came into the part of the steak house where he was sitting. Barry waved for him to come over to the booth where he sat.

"Hey, cheat, how are you doing?" Barry slurred.

"Looks to me you got started drinking a little early tonight. What are you doing here?"

"I'm here with Shay Everhart. I got big plans for her tonight. I know you couldn't get her into bed, but I'm going to show you how it is done." He laughed so loud several people turned and looked at him.

"Oh, is that so? I just saw her get in her car and drive out of the parking lot."

Barry had a stunned look on his face. "That bitch, she just came to dinner to see what she could find out."

"What do you mean?"

"She asked about the Z bar 3, but I was tightlipped and didn't tell her anything."

"Did you say anything about me being involved?"

"No, just that you were going to sell some of the time shares."

"I told her I was in for part of the action just to make her think I was in the big money to soften her up for the motel."

"You big dummy, when are you going to learn to keep your big mouth shut?"

"You can trust me. I didn't tell her any thing that I shouldn't."

"Did you tell her where the money came from?"

"No, no, how dumb do you think I am?"

"Pretty dumb."

"I told her you were a big operator and knew some big guys in California with a lot of cash they wanted to spend."

"I wished you could keep your mouth shut." He went on to use a lot of words that can't be printed. "Why didn't you just give her the whole layout with names, addresses, and phone numbers? I should just have my boys from Chicago teach you a lesson."

"No, no, you don't have to do that. I'll do anything you want me to."

"That you will. Shay already knows more than she should. I think she should be snuffed out, and I think you are the one to do it."

"Jippem, you know I can't do that. How about you have some of your boys do it? I'll pay whatever it costs."

"No, if you want to play on my team, you're going to learn to do what I tell you, and I want it done right away. Go ahead and have your fun with her and then get rid of her."

"Can't I have somebody else do it?"

"No, I want you to do it, and I want a video of you doing it just to make sure you did it yourself."

"Jippem, you are sick."

"I demand loyalty."

"How long do I have?"

"Two weeks max, and if I find out you've talked to anyone else, I'll have you taken care of, slow and painful." Jippem got up from the table and started to walk away.

"Wait, Jippem, I need a ride back to the office. My car is back there, and I came here with Shay."

"You can ride home with your wife. She's in the bar."

"What? I could have been caught with Shay. Lacey would have killed me."

"I'll send her in," said Jippem.

"No, you have to cover for me. Tell her I came here with you on business."

"Okay," he said and walked off. In a couple of minutes, Jippem was back with Lacey, walking with his arm around, her fondling her as he came with a big grin on his face. Jippem was obviously enjoying taking advantage of her as Barry watched, and she had enough drinks in her, so she didn't mind.

"Barry, what are you doing here?" she asked.

"Barry and I had some business to go over," chimed in Jippem.

"Can you give me a ride back to the office, dear? I left my car there."

"Sure, but let's go in the bar and have another drink."

"Sure, why not."

"I have to be going," said Jippem. "Remember our deal. I'll see you in the morning." He patted Lacey on the behind, making sure Barry saw him do it.

As Barry and his wife walked back into the bar, he said, "I don't like the way Jippem had his hands all over you."

"Oh, grow up. He's just a fat old man whose only enjoyment in life is us younger chicks. I know you have pretty loose hands when you have a few drinks."

"I do not. You know I am only faithful to you."

"Yeah, right, how about Trudy Welsh?"

"Well, maybe her, she's a hot chick." They stayed in the bar until closing time drinking, talking, arguing, and drinking some more. Barry was trying to forget the deal he and Jippem had. Could he get up the nerve to do it? He wasn't sure, but it was either her life or his. As he stumbled out to the car, holding on to Lacey's arm, he said, "Give me the keys, I'll drive. You're to drunk to sing." He laughed.

"No, I'll drive. You're to drunk to drive. You might scratch up my new car."

"Let's flip a coin to see who drives."

"I'll drive," said Lacey. "You already have two DUIs." As she backed out of her parking space, she nicked the car parked next to them, leaving a big scratch down one side. She drove onto the off ramp of Interstate 90 going the wrong way without lights. They drove right into oncoming traffic, and a screaming eighteen-wheeler bound for Seattle hit them head-on.

The local rescue squad and EMT's pried what was left of them out of the car with the jaws of life but too late to do any good. They had already gone straight to hell.

Shay didn't sleep very well that night and was happy she got the information she was after, but she was afraid of what Barry might do when he sobered up and realized how much he had told her. It was Saturday, and she and Sue always got together for breakfast, so she got ready and left her condo. Sue was already at Perkins when Shay showed up. When she walked up to the table, Shay said, "Hi, how are you this morning?" Sue didn't answer but pushed the morning newspaper she had been reading across the table to Shay. There on the front page was a picture of the worst accident she had ever seen. You could hardly tell it was a car.

"Man, that is some wreck," said Shay as she slid the paper back across the table.

"Read it," said Sue and pushed the paper back at her.

Shay started reading. "Barry Killmee! I had dinner with him last night."

"You what? Are you crazy? You're going to fool around until you get hurt?"

"Oh, stop worrying." Shay went on to explain what she had found out.

"You're not happy unless you're living on the edge, are you?" said Sue.

"Well, there's something funny going on out at the Z bar 3, and I am going to find out what it is."

"Is it worth getting killed over? The only reason you're doing it is that you're head over heels in love with this Dallas guy. When are you going to introduce him to me so I can tell you if he's worth it?"

"I am only doing it because it's the right thing to do, and I'm not head over heels in love with him. He's a nice guy and fun to be with, but we're not in love."

"Oh, I understand. That's why you spend more time out at the ranch than you do in town. That's the reason you haven't bothered to look for another job. It's because he's so much fun to be with. Go soak your head. I don't believe you for a minute. Why don't you just move out to the Z bar 3 and save all the gas running back and forth?"

"You're just jealous because you don't have a handsome man like Dallas."

"So now this 'friend only' is handsome?"

"Yes, he's handsome, polite, generous, considerate, respectful, well-mannered, gifted, elegant, God fearing, and sexy."

"And he's in love with Shay," added Sue.

"I wished he was. I've never met a man like him. He's so considerate, and he has never tried to take advantage of me. He's not like any other man I've ever been around." Shay had a tear in her eye.

"Does he know how you feel about him?"

"No, I've never told him."

"Why?"

"Because I'm not good enough for him."

"What makes you think that?"

"I don't know. He deserves the best girl in the world."

"You are the best girl in the world," Sue laid her hand over on Shay's.

"Thank you, Sue, I wished he felt that way."

"Ask him."

"Oh, I couldn't do that."

"Okay, I'll do it for you. What's his phone number?"

"You leave him alone. If you met him, I know you'd try and steal him from me."

"How could I steal him? I thought you said you didn't have him. Are there anymore like him out at the Z bar 3?"

"Yes, there are. The next time I go, maybe I'll take you with me, but you would have to promise not to say anything to Dallas about the way I feel about him."

"I promise. Just show me the guys."

CHAPTER EIGHTEEN

Shay was a prisoner in her own home, her own fears, and her own imagination. It started a week ago when she came home and listened to her voicemail.

"Shay, we know where you are, where you live, and where you are going. We'll get you! You know too much, and we are going to shut you up. Don't call the cops. We will be there before they are. Don't call your friends, or we'll take care of them too. Don't leave your condo, or we'll get you on the way. Just stay in your condo and worry! You don't have much food in your fridge, and that yogurt is out of date. Get rid of it. It's only a matter of time before you have to go out to get something to eat, and we'll be waiting. Who are we? You don't know, and you don't need to. We may be the guy next door. We may be the man in the phone booth down the street. We might be your neighbor next door who is mowing the lawn." She could hear a mower running, and she looked out the window. The guy next door was mowing his lawn. Who were they? Where were they? How did they know so much about her? "Don't go to the Z bar 3. We'll get you on the way. Don't call anyone. We are listening. Just enjoy your last remaining days. We will get you. Have a nice day."

That was day before yesterday, and Shay had not gone out or talked to anyone since. To say that Shay was scared would be an understatement. She didn't know what to do. Should she call somebody? Should she call the police? No, they said not to. Should she get in her car and drive to a place where there were a lot of people? Had they messed with her car so it wouldn't run? No, she had just driven up, and it was running okay then. Maybe she should turn around and get out of here, but where would she go? She was tired and needed some sleep, but that was easier said than done. Finally, she turned on the television, but out of almost two hundred channels, she couldn't find anything that interested her. She turned to *Fox News* and listened to them hash over the day's news for the umpteenth time. The news faded out, and she slept until three fifteen when a noise outside her window awoke her. She turned out all the lights, pulled back the curtain, and peered out into the night. She could see nothing out of the ordinary, but it was enough to keep her awake the rest of the night.

At six thirty she tried to eat something, but she wasn't hungry, and nothing looked good to her. She was surprised at how little food there was in the fridge. She looked at the yogurt, and it was outdated. How did they know? Had they been in her condo? She didn't notice anything missing or out of place, but they seemed to know a lot about her and where she lived. Were they really going to do something to her, or were they only trying to scare her? By the end of the day, she had decided to make a run for it. She didn't know how or when, but if she stayed here, she would go crazy. She put what she was going to need for a few days in two bags, no more than what she could carry in one load down to her car. Once she left the condo, she was not going to come back, ever.

She made up her mind that once she got in her car, she wasn't going to stop until she got to the ranch. She did have to stop for gas, but that was going to be it. She would keep a close eye to make sure she wasn't followed, and once she got to the interstate going east, she could outrun most anything on the road. Where was Dallas when she needed him? She would feel so safe if only she could be with him. If only she could be in his arms once more. The last time she left, he had told her to be safe and not get into trouble. He said, "Don't do anything I wouldn't do." And then he added, "I guess that gives you enough rope to hang yourself." Now here she was scared to death, and he didn't have any idea she was in trouble.

Why hadn't she listened to Dallas when he told her to just leave it alone? She wouldn't be in the trouble she was now. But then she wouldn't have the proof that something illegal was going on. When she started on this, she had no idea the money to buy the ranch was drug money that had to be put into something in order to clean it up. They could pour the cash into land and buildings and then sell shares to have money that was clean besides making a good profit on the project. Now she could see why they wanted the Z bar 3. There were over fifteen miles of lakeshore on one of the biggest and best fishing lakes in South Dakota. Barry had explained what the whole project was going to be like and all the money he was going to make on commissions and profit, being part-owner along with Jippem. Also she found out they would be using the airstrip for drug runs. Because of the tar runway in the middle of nowhere, jets from Colombia could land, dump their load, and be gone within minutes. There were no roads except the main one leading into the ranch. It would be easy to control who came and went. From there, the drugs could be loaded on other planes to be distributed to other parts of the upper Midwest, Minnesota, North and South Dakota, Nebraska, western Montana, and eastern Iowa. They were already doing business in these areas, but the distribution had been difficult.

Even though she was in trouble now, she was glad she had met with Barry. The more he had to drink, the drunker he got, and the drunker he got, the louder he got and the more he bragged. Then he got obnoxious and started pawing her. When she did get up to leave, the three guys at the next table asked if he was giving her trouble. They said they had overheard a lot and if she needed any witnesses to give them a call, and one of them gave her his business card. That was like striking gold. The case was building against Jippem and others, but she didn't know who they were. Barry and his wife had been killed, or they would have been in on it too.

The sheriff had located the pickup matching the tires where the cattle were shot but was waiting to arrest anyone until they had the whole case put together. He also had some leads that his brother had picked up in bars around the area concerning the fires. Evidence was coming together, but that didn't change the fact that Shay was still in trouble and didn't know what to do.

* * *

Dallas sat straight up in bed. Shay was in trouble. He knew it. He didn't know how, but it was real. Something wasn't right. Why had he let her go back to the city? He had had a bad feeling about it when she left, but she told him she was a big girl and could take care of herself. He didn't feel right about it, and he should never have let her go, but then who was he to order her around? He was sure that if she was in danger, it had something to do with all the trouble they had been having around the ranch—the cattle that were shot, the fire that was set, and also the dead cattle that they had found. He wasn't sure what had killed them. The report wasn't back from the university yet.

But then he remembered seeing her in the steak house with another guy. Maybe that was what woke him up. He had been upset about what was going on ever since that night. What had he been thinking? That Shay was his? She had never told him that she loved him. He knew how he felt about her and was hoping she felt the same way, but then Martha kept assuring him there was a good answer for her being at the restaurant. He had to admit he loved her and would do anything to win her back. *Shay where are you? Are you in trouble?*

He picked up the phone and called Shay. He knew she asked him not to, but this was important. He had to find out if she was okay. It rang until the voicemail picked up, but he didn't leave a message. He called again, still no answer. Then he dialed Sue's number.

A very sleepy voice said, "Hello."

"Sue, this is Dallas, Sorry I called so late, but I just woke up. I have a feeling something is wrong with Shay. I called her condo, but there was no answer. Have you seen her or talked to her in the last couple of days?"

"No, I haven't. What makes you think she's in trouble?"

"I really don't know, but you know how it is sometimes—you get a feeling something is wrong. You don't know why, but you're sure of it."

"Yes, I know what you mean. Do you want me to go over to her place and see if she's around or if something is wrong?"

"Let's see. It's five now. Why don't you wait an hour or so? I'm going to leave here right now, but it will take me a good three hours to get there."

Sue called Shay's phone, and when the voicemail picked up, she said, "Shay, pick up. It's me, Sue." But she didn't pick up. Shay heard her, but she was afraid to pick up the phone. The message had said they were listening, and she didn't want to talk to Sue. They may get the message that she was about to leave the condo, and besides, she didn't want to get Sue in trouble.

Sue tried again, still no answer. She got in her Jeep and drove over to Shay's apartment. Shay's car was in the drive, so she must be home. Taking two steps at a time to the second floor, she knocked on the door. She found it strange that no one answered the door as Shay stood on the other side and looked at the door in fear. She knocked again, "Shay, let me in. It's Sue." And she knocked again. All of a sudden, the door was jerked open and slammed shut the minute she was inside.

"What are you doing here, Sue?"

"Dallas called me out of his mind in fear, saying he was sure you were in big trouble and wanted me to come over to see if you were okay. He had called you and nobody answered."

"Dallas called you?"

"Yes, and he's on his way here to find out for himself, but he said it would take three hours or better to get here." Sue looked at Shay and saw the fear on her face. "What's wrong, what's going on?" she asked. Shay spent the next half hour telling Sue about the voicemail and the details of her meeting with Barry. She had told her most of this before, but she was so nervous she had to go over it all again.

"What do you think I should do?' Shay asked.

"Do you think they're really out to harm you, or are they just trying to scare you so you will keep your mouth shut?"

"I don't know, but it's driving me crazy just sitting here wondering when they're coming to get me and what they might do to me."

"What do you want to do?"

"I really want be at the Z bar 3 in Dallas's arms. I feel so safe whenever I'm with him."

"Well then, that's where I think you should go."

"Will you go with me?"

"Sure, I have been wanting you to take me there for weeks. I want to meet all those cute cowboys you told me about." Sue grinned.

"Okay," said Shay, "I had already made up my mind to make a run for it. I figure if I can get to the interstate before they get me, I can outrun them and make it to the ranch before they catch me. I already have my bags packed."

"What if they've done something to your car?"

"Then we will take your Jeep."

"Why wouldn't we take my Jeep in the first place?"

"Because my car is faster. We couldn't outrun anybody with your Jeep."

"Well, let's do it," said Sue.

Shay picked up her bags, looked around the condo, and headed for the door. Sue opened the door, and the two of them ran down the steps out into the early morning air. Shay threw her bags in the backseat and jumped in behind the wheel. As she turned the key, the engine turned over a couple of times and roared to life. She backed out of the drive and made a quick survey of the surrounding area and saw nothing out of the ordinary, but she still left the condo at more than the posted speed.

Heading for the interstate, she took the streets she knew were the fastest, and at every light, she looked to see if there was anybody who looked like they may be watching them. With one eye on the road ahead and one eye on the rearview mirror, she drove as fast as she dared. Just as they got to the interstate, she said to Sue, "I'm going to pull in here for gas. Why don't you go inside and get us some coffee?"

Shay swiped her credit card at the pump and started filling her car with high-test gasoline. She surveyed the other customers and kept an eye on anybody that was coming and going from the station. Two pumps over was a car with two men. One was putting in gas, and the other one kept looking in her direction. Was he keeping an eye on her, or was it just her imagination? The pump clicked off just as Sue came out. When she put the hose back on the pump, she once again looked over at the two guys, and neither one was looking her way. She took her time in pulling away from the pumps, hoping the two guys would leave first, and then she would know for sure whether they had been watching her or not. The two men pulled out of the station, and with relief, she followed. With her blinker on, she turned toward the interstate. The two guys were about half a block ahead of her when they pulled over to the curb, and she passed them.

When she pulled onto the on-ramp heading east on I-90, she was sure that nobody was behind them. Running up to about seventy-five miles per hour, she looked over at Sue and said, "I think we made it out of town without anyone behind us."

"I'm not too sure."

"What do you mean?"

"That Ford pickup behind us was at the station when we got gas."

"The white one or the red one?" Shay asked as she looked in the mirror.

"The white one."

"Yeah, I saw them at the station, but it was a man and a woman."

"So?"

"I guess I was so intent on the car with two men that I didn't pay any attention to that pickup."

"Slow down and see if they pass us."

Shay slowed down and so did the pickup, so she sped up, and they stayed right with them. She really stepped on it until she was well over ninety, and they were right behind her.

"I'm going to slow way down and you see if you can read their license number. Are you ready?" Shay asked.

"Yep."

Shay slammed on the brakes, and the pickup had to swerve to miss her, but Sue said, "I got it." The truck still didn't pass them.

"I'm going to try something else. Hang on when we come to the next exit."

They continued on east for several miles before they came to the next exit. Just before they got to it, Shay slammed on the brakes again, and the pickup had to swerve to the left to keep from hitting her. At the last minute, Shay swung to the right, heading up the off-ramp, and so did the pickup, cutting up through the ditch but staying behind her. She went through the stop sign at the top of the ramp and down the other side back onto the interstate with the truck right behind her.

"You're right. They are following us."

"You must be kidding. You had to go through all that just to make sure?"

"Yes, I did."

"What are we going to do?" asked Sue.

"Try to get Dallas on the cell phone again. He has to be in range pretty soon."

Sue dialed his number. "It still didn't go through."

"Let's see if we can outrun them."

Shay put the pedal to the metal, and before she knew it, she was up around 130 miles per hour, and they watched the pickup fade in the distance.

"There, I guess that did it," said Shay, and she slowed to a more reasonable speed.

"There's always a speed trap up here a few miles. No use giving the State of South Dakota any more money than I have already."

"How do you know?"

"Oh, I've donated a time or two."

A few exits farther east a, car came off the on-ramp and pulled up behind them. Shay kept an eye on them in her rearview mirror.

"Sue, don't look now, but there has been a car following us for the last few miles."

"Just outrun them too."

"I've been up over a hundred, and they stay right with us."

"The speed trap is coming up at the next exit. I am going to try something. You won't see anything, but if you look close, there will be somebody in the middle of the bridge with a radar gun, and there will be patrol cars on the other side high up on the on ramp. Just hold on."

Shay slowed to about seventy, and the car behind her did the same thing. They wouldn't pick her up for speeding. The car behind pulled up alongside of them, and the guy in the passenger's seat pointed a gun in their direction.

"Shay, he's got a gun!" hollered Sue as she ducked down in the seat.

Shay locked up the brakes and pulled the wheel to the right. There was a screeching of tires, and you could smell the burning rubber as she left a lot of tire on the concrete. The Mustang went into a slide, and she did a complete 180 on the pavement. The car with the gunman went shooting right past them, missing them by inches. When Shay was all the way around, she straightened the wheel, dumped the brakes, hit the gas, and went roaring through the ditch back onto the on-ramp, going the wrong way. She headed past the police cars onto the crossroad and slid to a stop in the midst of flying gravel, dust, and running police officers.

In the meantime, the car that had been following turned around and came back down the interstate on the wrong side of the road, and when they saw the police cars, they kept right on going. The minute she stopped, there were several cops around the car, all with guns drawn, pointing in her direction. Two others went flying down the off-ramp after the other car. One of the patrolmen hollered, "Let me see your hands! Keep them up in the air!" Both Shay and Sue put their hands up so the cops could see them. The doors were opened and the troopers stepped back.

"Get out of the car," they ordered. "Keep your hands over your head." Shay and Sue did as they were told.

"Lie across the hood," said one of the cops as he came up behind them and cuffed their hands behind their backs. "Okay, turn around." The one officer looked at Shay and said, "Didn't I give you a ticket for speeding just a couple of weeks ago."

"Yes, sir."

"What are you trying to do, kill yourselves along with us?"

"No, sir."

"Where in the world did you learn to drive. I have never seen a woman turn a car around like that going over seventy miles an hour."

"I have an uncle who is a patrolman. He taught me, sir."

"What are you trying to do, kill yourself?"

"No, sir, but those guys in that other car were trying to kill us. They pointed a gun at us."

"What?"

"They pointed a gun at us when they passed us."

"Charley, get on the horn and tell Bill that the other car is carrying."

"Take the cuffs off these two," the sergeant said to one of the other officers. "I guess they're only dangerous to themselves."

Dallas had tried to call Shay several times, but she must have her cell phone off, so he tried Sue and he couldn't get her either. He was over halfway to Rapid City when up ahead, he saw red lights flashing, so he slowed to just five miles over the speed limit. He didn't want to be held up by the police, and besides he didn't want to pay a speeding ticket. As he looked to see what was going on, he spotted Shay's car. What in the world did the cops have her stopped for? Why was she off on the exit? Surely she hadn't tried to outrun them. Down the road about three miles, he saw the Highway Patrol had another car stopped, and it looked like he was going the wrong way. There were two guys lying on the ground out in front of the car and one of the officers had a gun on them. Dallas went to the next overpass where he turned around and headed back east. He pulled off on the overpass where he thought he saw Shay's car, and when he came up to the stop sign, sure enough it was her. One of the patrolmen waved him to either turn or go on, but he pulled to the shoulder and got out. The patrolman pulled his gun and hollered, "Put your hands in the air! What do you want?" Shay looked up and couldn't believe her eyes. It was Dallas.

"That's a friend of mine. He isn't going to hurt anybody."

"What in the world is going on here? We set up a little speed trap, and all of a sudden, we got everybody in the county here. This would be a good place to set up a coffee shop."

Shay ran over to Dallas and flew into his arms, and he held her. "Are you all right, dear? I was so worried about you."

"Yes, I am now that you're here. I was so scared. How did you know I was in trouble? I will never ever do anything you tell me not to again."

The police sergeant walked up. "It looks like you must know this girl," he said to Dallas. "You better get her off the road before she kills herself. She just did a power turn in the middle of the highway like a professional."

"You did what?'

"I just turned around and came back to where these guys were."

"She turned around at seventy-three miles an hour. I haven't got a man on the force who can do that," chimed in the officer.

"Shay, you could have been killed."

"Not if you know what you're doing."

"I'm sorry, Officer," said Dallas as he stuck out his hand. "I'm Dallas Ziglar, and I will keep her off the road until she learns to drive."

The officer held on to Dallas's hand and looked at him. "Dallas Ziglar from the Z bar 3?" he asked.

"Yes."

"I've been working on some of your problems out there with Sheriff Coldsted. I think we're about ready to make some arrests in that case."

"Sarge, Bill wants to talk to you on the radio!" hollered Charley.

"Excuse me. By the way, I'm Sergeant Williams. You better take this girl home."

Shay turned to Sue, "Oh, I'm sorry, Sue. This is Dallas. She's my best friend, Dallas, Sue."

"Wow, he's even better looking than you said he was," she said as she shook his hand. "If you ever decide to dump Shay, give me a ring."

"It's not a matter of me dumping her. She may just dump me." He looked at Shay without a smile. Shay looked at Dallas without saying anything. He was serious. What did he mean?

"You guys go on ahead to the ranch," said Dallas. "I talked to Sheriff Jim on the way here, and he wanted me to stop. I told him I had to go to Rapid City first, but I promised to stop on the way back. I don't know how long it will take."

Shay really wanted to ride with Dallas, but she didn't ask any questions. She got in her car, and she and Sue headed for the ranch. Dallas seemed indifferent after he found out she was safe. What was going on, or was it that he was under so much stress?

It only took a little over an hour for them to get to the ranch, but the last thirty minutes or so, Sue started asking questions like, "How much farther is it? Did you take the wrong road? Are you sure you know where you're going? This must be two miles on the other side of nowhere."

When they came to the sign "YOU ARE NOW ENTERING THE Z bar 3 RANCH," she said, "Finally we're here." Shay didn't say anything but just kept driving.

After a couple of miles, Sue asked, "Where are the buildings? I thought the sign said we were entering the ranch."

"Oh, it's a way yet." Then they came to the main gate, and Sue said, "So have we arrived?"

"Pretty soon." Another two miles, and they topped the hill where they could see the buildings and the river in the background.

"There it is," said Shay.

"Wow, it's beautiful and so big. I didn't know there was a lodge here."

"That's not a lodge. It's the main house."

"Really?"

They stopped in front of the main house, and Shay started to get out. "We'll get the bags later. You might as well stay overnight."

"But I didn't bring anything."

"That's okay. We'll fix you up."

Shay opened the front door and hollered, "Martha, you home?"

"Don't you even knock?"

"No, Martha wouldn't like it."

Martha came hurrying into the great room, wiping her hands on her apron. "Oh, Shay, I'm so glad to see you." She threw her arms around Shay's neck. "Did you see Dallas? He was so worried that something had happened to you."

"Yes, we met him on the road. Martha, I want you to meet my best friend. This is Sue. Sue, this is Martha. She runs the place with an iron hand."

"Don't listen to Shay;" said Martha. "I'm only the cook and housekeeper."

"That's not true. She takes care of Dallas like he's her little boy. She has him so spoiled that it's just terrible."

"Come in, girls. I was just about ready to sit down and have some lunch. It's not much, but it will tide you over till dinner." She brought out some potato salad, coleslaw, a plate of lunch meats and cheese, and a plate of sliced fruit. She also set out some bread, butter, and the works. "Save room for pie," she said.

Sue looked at the table in disbelief. "This is no lunch. This is a banquet."

Shay smiled. "Wait until dinner. Martha doesn't know when to quit." After a long lunch of eating and talking to Martha, Shay showed Sue around the house and the ranch.

"If you don't grab this guy and soon, I'm just going to shoot you to get you out of the way and grab him myself."

"Sue, we're just friends."

"Right and you're stupid."

CHAPTER NINETEEN

It was late, way too late, when Shay saw the headlights of Dallas's pickup coming over the hill just west of the ranch. She had been waiting for him for the past several hours. Why didn't he come? Was something wrong? She sensed that things weren't right when he told her and Sue to go on to the ranch. She had sent Sue to bed an hour or so ago and told her that she was going to wait up for Dallas.

Shay stepped out onto the porch as she watched him come closer. She wanted to run out to meet him, but something held her back. He drove right on past the house, down to one of the shops, backed up to the big door, and got out. She left the porch and walked down to the shop. She looked in the open door and saw him sitting by one of the work benches just staring off into space. Shay stopped in the doorway and just watched him for a minute. "What are you doing?" she asked.

He whirled around at the sound of her voice. "What are you doing here?" he asked.

"I was waiting for you to come home."

"Why?"" There was a distinct chill as he spoke.

"I wanted to see you, but I sense that you didn't want to see me."

He dropped his head and said nothing.

"Dallas?" She waited. Finally he looked up. There were tears in his eyes.

"Dallas, what's wrong?" she asked as she walked closer.

"Do you love me?" he asked and then waited.
"Why do you ask? You've never asked that before?"
"Do you love me?"
"Yes, I love you."
"What about that guy I saw you with in Rapid the other night?"
"What guy?"
"Last Wednesday at the Wagon Wheel Steak House."
"How did you know I was there?"
"I saw you there."
"What were you doing there?"
"I came to town to surprise you and take you out to dinner. I was the one who got the surprise. There you were out with another guy, and I thought I knew you better than that. The least you could've done is tell me you were seeing other guys, so I wouldn't make a fool of myself."

"DALLAS, STOP!" He looked at her with a surprised look on his face.

"I love you! I never told you that before, but I do love you. Yes, I was out with another guy, but I did it for you."

"For me?"

"Yes, for you, you big dummy, and I almost got myself killed because of it. I ran into Barry Killmee, the guy you were going to drag into town. He asked me out for dinner. I didn't want to go, but I thought this was my chance to get some information out of him. Well, of course he started drinking, which I knew he would, and the more he drank, the mouthier he got. Then he started to brag to impress me. The whole idea was to get me into bed later on that night. You know how guys are."

"Were you drinking too?"

"Dallas! I'm not even going to answer that. I'm a Christian now."

"I'm sorry."

"By the end of the evening, he told me that they wanted to buy the ranch to make a time share out of it. The whole reason they want to do that is to launder some drug money. They were also going to use the airstrip to bring in drugs from Colombia and then distribute them to the surrounding states. The big money was coming out of California, but Jippem and Barry are involved too. Well, not Barry anymore, he and his wife were killed that night in a traffic accident."

"How did you get away from him?"

"Well, about nine o'clock, after I got as much information as I thought I could, I excused myself to go to the little girl's room. I left and went home."

"What time did you say you left?"

"About nine, I think."

"I must have just missed you. I left the parking lot for home at just a few minutes before nine." said Dallas.

"It was a couple of days later that I got the phone call telling me that they knew where I was and that they were going to get me. I was so scarred." Dallas got up from where he was sitting and walked past Shay to the open door. He stood there, looking at the moon. Shay just stood there and watched him without saying a word. After a while, she walked over and stood beside him. He was crying.

"I'm sorry, Dallas. I didn't mean to hurt you. I thought I was doing the right thing, and I wanted so much to find out what was going on. I just wanted to help because you already had enough pressure with the mortgage and everything."

"It's not you. I'm the big jerk. I should have trusted you, but I came into town and was so looking forward to spending the evening with you. When I looked in through the window and saw you sitting there with another guy, at first, I couldn't believe it. I was brokenhearted, and then I was mad. I was so afraid of losing you even though I had never told you I loved you or wanted you. I still considered you my girl." Shay reached over and put her arm around him but didn't say anything. "I'm supposed to be a strong Christian, but I didn't even think of praying, for myself or for you. I keep telling you that all things will work together for good to them that love God, and I wanted you to believe it, but I didn't believe it myself. When I came home and told Martha and Hank you were with another guy, she defended you. She said maybe it was your brother or cousin or something. She said you had a good reason for being there. Did I believe her? No, I thought the worst of you."

"Dallas! Stop! Stop beating up on yourself. I would've felt the same way if I had seen you out with another woman. Only I would have probably come in and slapped whoever you were with and dragged you out of the steak house."

"Do you really feel that way about me?"

"Yes, I do. Why else do you think I would risk getting killed? It's because I love you. If I would have listened to you and not tried to fix everything myself, I wouldn't have been in this situation. I'm so sorry. You know I wasn't with Barry because I wanted to be, don't you?"

"It's not you. I'm the one who should be sorry."

"Let's make a deal. I'll be sorry for hurting you, and you can be sorry for not trusting me. Then we'll just forget it, okay?"

"That's a deal." He took her in his arms and held her.

"Dallas?" she said in a dreamy voice.

"Yes."

"Why is the moon so much prettier out here than any other place in the world?"

"It isn't. It's just that you see it through different eyes."

"Can we walk up to the bench that overlooks the Missouri?"

So hand in hand, they walked through the evening darkness the quarter of a mile to the bluff that overlooked the river and sat down on the bench that his grandfather had put there years ago. They sat and talked about the things that had just happened and what the future looked like.

"The sheriff wants to meet with us tomorrow. He has a lot of leads, and he wants to compare them with things that you know. He thinks they're about to make some arrests. He wants to make sure that they get the big guys, and not just the small players. He knows who shot the cattle and set the fires, but he's still not sure about the cattle that were poisoned. The tests still aren't back yet. The bad thing about arresting these guys is I no longer have a sale for the ranch. I still have the mortgage that's due pretty soon, and if I don't come up with the money, I will lose everything. If I would have sold to those guys, at least, I would have had a little money leftover to start some place else. Not very much but some."

"Oh right, I can just see you taking drug money and starting over again and being happy."

"I guess you're right. How do you always know what I should do? You make me think that I can't get along without you."

"That's what I am trying to get you to think."

It was late when they got back to the house. "Do you want a snack before you go to bed, maybe a couple of cookies and a glass of milk?"

"Sure, why not?"

As they sat around the kitchen table, Dallas thought to himself that it was sure good to have Shay there with him again. It would be really easy to get used to this, but the future didn't look good for either them or the ranch. Only a few days more and he was going to have to either come up with the money for the mortgage or give up the ranch. That would be real hard to do, but he really didn't have much choice.

They climbed the log stairway hand in hand, and when they reached the top, Shay said, "The master bedroom is this way."

"Are you trying to tempt me?"

"No, it wouldn't work with you. You're too strong, and I was just teasing."

"I would say some day, but the future is so uncertain."

"For we know that all things work together for good."

"Yes, I know Shay. Sometimes I wish I was as strong as you are."

When they reached Shay's bedroom door, she turned to him and asked, "Do I get a good-night kiss?" He took her in his arms and kissed her like he had never kissed her before.

When she caught her breath, she asked, "What was that all about?" He didn't answer but went on down the hall to his room and closed the door. Shay stepped into her room and dropped on her knees beside the bed.

"Lord," she prayed, "be very close to Dallas right now. He's under so much stress, and I know it's hard for him to understand why you haven't shown him what he should do or how you are going to come to his rescue. No matter how it turns out, I know it will be for the best, and we will still love and follow you. Amen." She got up from her knees and, as she got ready for bed, she had peace in her heart. She loved the Lord and she loved Dallas.

Just two doors down the hall, Dallas was on his knees, talking to the Lord and saying almost the same thing that Shay was saying. "Lord, I'm leaving it all in your hands. I trust you and love you. Be with Shay. I love her and need her, but I also need to be able to support her. Your will be done. Amen."

CHAPTER TWENTY

The birds were singing outside of Shay's window when she woke up. She looked out the window, and the sun was high in the sky. She looked at the clock, eight thirty. Why didn't the alarm go off? Did she forget to set it? She was so taken back by the good-night kiss that Dallas had given her that she couldn't think straight. She hurriedly showered and dressed and went downstairs. Martha was standing at the kitchen sink, doing what Shay assumed were the breakfast dishes.

"Good morning," she said in a sheepish voice, "I guess I kind of overslept."

"That's good," said Martha. "Dallas told me what you've gone through the last few days. I knew something was wrong because the other night I woke up, and the Lord told me to pray for you. You can't stay in the city any longer. You have to come out here until this all blows over."

"I would feel a lot safer out here, but I'm not sure Dallas would put up with me."

"We don't care what Dallas wants," replied Martha, "but you can't stay in Rapid City. Here, sit down. The coffee is still hot, and I will quick-fry you a couple of eggs."

"No, just a cup of coffee and some toast is fine, but I can get it myself. Where is everybody this morning?"

"Dallas went up to one of the north pastures to check on some cattle, and Sue is bothering Rusty down by one of the corrals. She seems to think he is awfully nice."

"Dallas told me not to let you go until he got back. When are the two of you getting married?"

"He hasn't asked me."

"Don't wait for that. He's a proud man and won't ask you until he's sure he can give you all the finer things in life. This mortgage business really has put him under a lot of stress."

"I don't want the finer things of life. I only want him."

"I know that and you know that, but does he know that? It may boil down to you asking him."

"I couldn't do that. He already thinks I'm too bossy."

"I would rather live in a shack with Dallas than in a mansion with somebody I didn't love."

"If you feel that way, you've found the right man. That's the way I feel about Hank."

"I really don't know what to do," said Shay.

About that time, Dallas came in through the back door, "You don't know what to do about what? You could start by getting up in the morning. If you didn't stay up all night, you would be able to start when the rest of us do. I just don't understand these city girls."

"If I didn't have to go out and find you to make sure you got back to the house, I could go to bed at a decent time. I was afraid you might've got lost," answered Shay. "Have you seen Sue? We have to get back to Rapid City. I think she has to go to work this afternoon."

"Right, you're not going back to town until I can go with you, then only to get what you need to stay here until these guys that are after you are in jail. Most guys I know only have to worry about somebody stealing their girl, but no, I have to worry about mine getting shot."

"Since when did I become your girl?"

"When you couldn't take care of yourself."

"Don't worry. I'll be all right. They got the guys who were after me."

"That's right. They got the guys who tried to shoot you, but they didn't get the guy who told them to do it."

"Dallas, you're making a mountain out of a molehill."

"Shay! I have a couple of things I have to do. You're not going anywhere until I say you can and I can go with you."

Dallas was not smiling, and she knew he meant it. "Yes, dear, I won't go until you say its okay."

"That's more like it.' And he put his arm around her before he walked out the door.

"I don't know why I put that man through so much grief," she said to Martha. "If I would have listened to him in the first place, I wouldn't be in all this trouble."

"You do it because you are headstrong, self-sufficient, and fully capable of taking care of yourself, and if you weren't all those things, Dallas wouldn't be at all interested in you. He likes a woman that can think for herself and isn't afraid to make a decision."

"I've noticed that. When I'm right, he isn't intimidated or afraid to say so. But when he's right, he won't let me talk him out of it. I've never met a man quite like Dallas."

"There aren't any men like Dallas," said Martha. "He's one of a kind and is just like a son to Hank and me."

It wasn't long before Dallas had his jobs done and was ready to leave for Rapid City.

"Where in the world is Sue? Doesn't she remember she has a job?" Shay asked.

"Last I saw her, she was sitting on the corral rail, watching Rusty breaking a gelding. He was putting on quite a show, and I think he was trying to impress her," Dallas responded.

"I don't think it would take much," said Shay. "She was pretty taken in by his looks. Plus I don't know that she's ever met anyone as polite as he is. "I'll go down and get her."

As she walked up to where Sue was sitting, Shay said, "Are you about done being impressed? We have to get going."

"I don't want to go. This is too much fun."

"But don't you have to go to work this afternoon?"

"No, not until tomorrow afternoon."

"Well, I guess you can stay here if you want to. Dallas and I are going back into Rapid. He wants me to get some things and come stay at the ranch until the guys who are after me are in jail."

"That sounds like a setup deal. Why don't you just marry the guy and then you can stay here all the time?"

"He hasn't asked me, and besides, if he did ask me, I'm not sure that I would marry him."

"Well, if you aren't going to marry him, let me know so I can go after him. He would be a real good catch."

"What about Rusty?"

"Isn't he a darling though? I think I could get to like him."

As Shay walked into the kitchen, she said, "Is it okay if Sue stays here while we're gone? I couldn't get her to come."

"Sure," said Martha, "I'll keep an eye on her so Rusty doesn't run off with her."

"Let's take my pickup," said Dallas. "Nobody will be looking for you in a pickup, and then you can bring more stuff than you could fit in your car. I know how women are—they always need more things than a man would ever need."

"I wouldn't talk if I were you. I've looked in your closet a time or two."

Just after they hit the interstate, they pulled into a truck stop to get some fuel and something to eat. As she sat there, sipping her coffee she didn't say a word but was just enjoying looking at Dallas. He was rugged but handsome. His bushy, curly hair sticking out from under his hat, and his deep blue eyes explained why she was so taken in by this man.

"What?" he said.

"I didn't say anything."

"Why are you looking at me then?"

"Would you rather I look at some other guy?"

"No, but why are you looking at me?"

"Because you're so handsome even if you did forget to shave."

He put his hand up to his chin. "You're right. I did. Some woman kept me up so late last night that I didn't get up in time to shave."

"From now on, I'll see that you're in bed by ten o'clock."

"That doesn't sound like any fun."

About that time, their food came, and they went right to work on it. They were both hungry. The waitress brought the coffeepot and check and asked, "Is there anything else that I can get you?"

"Do you want some dessert, Shay?"

"No, I'm fine."

"I guess that's all," Dallas told the waitress. "Thank you."

Shay picked up the check, and Dallas said, "Here, give that to me."

"I got it. It's my turn."

"No, Shay, give it to me."

"Are you hard of hearing? I said I would get it. It's all right for the girl to treat once in a while. I know you big he-men think you should always pay, but I have a job, or had a job, and I'm not broke yet."

After they got back on the road, Dallas said, "That door doesn't latch very good. Maybe you should slide over by me. I wouldn't want you to fall out."

She slid over, and he put his arm around her. "That's much better." It was good being together, and before they knew it, they were coming into the city.

When they walked into Shay's condo, she noticed the light on the answering machine was flashing, so she poked the button to get the messages. *Click.*

"Hi, baby. Give me a call right away. It's very important."

"That's Daddy," said Shay.

Click.

"Shay, you outfoxed those two guys, but we'll still get you."

There were just the two messages. She threw her arms around Dallas. "I'm so glad you made me wait and not come alone," she said. "I better call Daddy."

"Here, use my cell in case they have your phone bugged."

She started dialing his office phone just as her phone started to ring. Dallas looked at Shay and then at the phone and reached over and picked it up, "Hello."

"Do I have the right number? Is Shay Everhart there?"

"Who's calling please?"

"This is Wilson Everhart, her father."

"Just a minute please," Dallas covered the receiver and said to Shay, "Is your father's name Wilson?"

"Yes," she said, and Dallas handed her the receiver.

"Hi, Daddy."

"Who answered the phone?"

"Just a friend of mine, and he's very protective."

"That's good. I like him already, whoever he is."

"I didn't want to leave a message that's why I wanted you to call me back. Have you been gone?"

"Yes, I was out to Dallas's ranch. Dallas is the man that answered the phone.

"Oh, I see. Is there something I should know?"

"No, Daddy. Don't worry, I'm a big girl."

"Okay, the reason I called was to tell you your Aunt Grace died yesterday from a brain aneurysm."

"Oh no, how is Mom taking it?"

"She was pretty shocked, but she's handling it very well."

"She hadn't been sick, had she?"

"No, it was totally unexpected."

"I'll come right home. I'll see if I can get a flight out this afternoon."

"That would be great. Jim is in South America with the plane, or I would have him come and get you."

"No, it will be faster this way. Hope to see you in a few hours. Tell Mom I'm praying for you guys, bye."

Shay turned to Dallas. "Mom's sister Grace died yesterday from a brain aneurysm. She was only fifty-two."

"I'm so sorry," said Dallas as he took her in his arms.

"I have to get to Houston as soon as I can."

"Sure," he said, "I'll take you to the airport right away. Do you have to pack anything?"

"I'll just throw some things in a bag. I have a lot of clothes at home, but I'll probably have to buy something for the funeral."

They went to the airport, and as luck would have it, she could get right on a flight to Kansas City and, from there, a direct flight to Houston. She would be there at six eighteen this evening. Dallas held her close and gently kissed her on the top of the head.

"Before I let you go, you have to make me a promise. Promise me, you will come back," Dallas said.

She tipped her head up and looked at him, "I promise." And their lips met in a lingering kiss. Then she was gone. That was the hardest thing he had ever done—watching her walk out of sight and disappear through the door leading to the plane. Would she come back? Oh, he knew she would. Would she call, or should he call her? Could he get by for a few days without talking to her? It was going to be hard. He missed her already as he watched her plane taxi out to the end of the runway and take off. He stood there and watched until he could no longer see the plane and then slowly walked out of the terminal to his truck.

When Shay got off the plane in Houston, her dad and mother were there waiting for her. There were the usual hugs and greetings. It was so good to see them again, and they seemed so happy.

"I need to make a phone call before we leave," she said as she pulled up the number in the memory on her cell.

"Hello," came the answer on the other end of the line.

"Hi, cowboy, it's me. I just wanted to let you know I made it okay. I know how you worry."

"I'm so glad you called. I've been thinking about you."

"Good, I don't want you to forget me."

"Mom and Daddy were here to pick me up. They are waiting, so I'll let you go. Don't get into any trouble while I'm gone. Bye."

"Bye," he wanted to say more, but this was not the time.

"Was that the guy who answered the phone when I called? Dallas, I think you said? Do you have a live-in now?"

"No, Daddy, we're just friends, and besides, I wouldn't let anybody move in with me unless we were married."

"Good, I'm glad to hear that."

They stopped to have supper on the way home and talked until about midnight, catching up on what was happening in one another's life. Shay's dad got up and went in the kitchen to get a snack, and her mom said to Shay, "You look so good, so happy."

"I am happy, Mom. I've met two real good friends."

"Yes, I know. This Dallas and who else?"

"Jesus Christ."

"Dad!" Shay's mother hollered. "Come here quick."

Wilson came running from the kitchen. "What is it?"

"Darling, tell Dad what you just told me."

"What?"

"Tell him the other friend you met."

"Jesus Christ," Shay responded.

"Oh, darling," Wilson said as he came and threw his arms around her, "that makes me so happy."

"I don't understand," said Shay.

"Your mother and I met him too about a month ago."

"Really? How?"

"Do you know who Joel Osteen is?"

"No. Oh, maybe I do. Isn't he on TV?"

"Yes, he's the pastor, our pastor of Lakewood Church," said her mother. "Dad had some business dealings with him, and to make a long story short, Pastor Joel led Dad to the Lord, and then your father came home and led me to the Lord. We have been so happy ever since. We are going to Lakewood, and we want you to go with us on Sunday."

"Man, I can hardly believe you and Dad are Christians. That makes me so happy."

"Well we're happy for you too. How did it happen?"

"I went out to the Z bar 3 to see if I could get the owner to sell. The real estate company I worked for had a buyer for that ranch. But the owner didn't want to sell it. This guy and the people who worked for him were so happy and were so content. Even though he had a big mortgage hanging over his head, he was at peace. He never preached to me but just lived his life, and I wanted what he had. So one day I asked the woman who does the cooking—Martha is her name, the sweetest lady you have ever met—about it, and she led me to the Lord."

"The owner of this ranch doesn't happen to be Dallas, does it?"

"Yes, he is such a nice guy."

"He hasn't asked you to marry him, has he?"

"No, he wouldn't do that without talking to Daddy first. He's just that kind of guy."

"So he is a rancher?"

"Yes, the prettiest place you've ever seen."

"What size ranch is it?" her dad asked.

"Forty-eight thousand acres."

"Wow, that's big. You say he has a big mortgage?"

"Yes, his father bought a big chunk of land to add to the ranch before he and his mother were killed in a plane accident and then the cattle prices went to pieces, and it has been real dry, so he's had to buy a lot of hay and couldn't pay off the mortgage."

"What do you think he will do about it?"

"I don't know. He says the Lord will provide."

"I like that. He must really trust in the Lord. How much is the mortgage?"

"Two and a half million."

"I think the Lord will take care of it," said her father. Wilson looked at his watch. "Oh my, it's almost one o'clock, and we need to get to bed. We can talk more in the morning."

"Your bedroom is all ready," said Shay's mom. "I'll see you in the morning."

Shay went to her room, and as she got ready for bed, she wondered if it was too late to call Dallas. She didn't care how late it was. She just had to tell him the good news. She dialed his number, and after several rings, she heard a sleepy *hello* on the other end.

"Hi, cowboy, were you sleeping?"

"Yes, what time is it anyway?"

"Almost one, but I just had to talk to you. I'm sorry to wake you."

"Oh, that's okay. I had to get up to answer the phone anyway."

"Darling, I got here to Houston and found out that both Mom and Dad have given their hearts to Jesus! Isn't that wonderful?"

"Oh, Shay, I am so happy for you. I know you've been praying for them. I'm so glad you called and told me."

"I'll let you get back to sleep. I just had to tell you."

"Oh no, you don't. You woke me up now. You're going to talk to me. I miss you so much." They talked for a long time before saying good night and going to sleep with each other, eleven hundred miles apart.

The next few days were busy with funeral plans, family meetings, and just meeting with friends and relatives. Shay hadn't been home for several months, and there were people she wanted to meet besides all the relatives who had come in from all over the United States. The funeral was sad. There was no hope. Aunt Grace was not a Christian, and her eternal home did not look good. The preacher did his best trying to preach her into heaven, but Shay knew in her heart that she didn't make it. After the funeral, there was a big lunch and get-together and, after that, quietness. Everyone went their separate ways, and Shay went home with her folks. It was good to just kick off her high heels and curl up on the couch and watch TV. Her mother was in the kitchen just fiddling and thinking of the good times she had enjoyed with her sister. Her dad was in the den reading. Shay looked at her watch. It was seven fifty-five. Was Dallas in the house yet? She hadn't talked to him since the time they spent together on the phone in the middle of the night. She dialed the ranch number.

"Hello, Z bar 3."

"Hi, Martha, it's me, Shay. Are you keeping busy?"

"Well, hello, Shay, how is your mom?"

"Oh, she's doing all right. Did Dallas tell you that when I got here, I found out that both my mom and dad had given their hearts to the Lord?"

"Yes, he did! He was so happy for you."

"Is he around?"

"Yes, he's in the office, wasting time. Just a minute, I'll call him."

When he picked up the phone, he said, "Hi, cutey, I'm glad you called. I thought you might have forgotten about me."

"Not on you life. I'm sorry I didn't call sooner. I've been so busy with the funeral and all the family and friends that were around. We never got home until late, and I didn't want to call then. I got you up late one night and that was enough."

"I didn't mind. You can call me any time, day or night. Did you meet a lot of old friends and relatives?"

"Yes, I sure did. I saw relatives I haven't seen in years. I met some of my old high school classmates, and I even saw my old boyfriend, Jim Carter."

Dallas was very quiet.

"What's wrong? That didn't bother you, did it?"

"Did it bother you?" he asked.

"Dallas! Stop it. He's a nice guy but not as nice as the one I have on the Z bar 3."

"Maybe you should reconsider, knowing I almost got you killed, and besides, our future together is very questionable. I don't know what my future is. I met with the bankers this afternoon and begged them for more time on the note, but they said they couldn't do that. They said they were going to start foreclosure next week. I told them they didn't have to do that if I didn't have the money by next week. I would just sign the ranch over to them."

"What happened to all things work together for good?"

"It's still in place, but evidently, me keeping the ranch is not the good that the Lord has planned for me."

"For you or for us?"

"Shay, I wanted it to be us. I really did, but I don't have anything to offer you. You've been in trouble ever since you met me. You had to quit your job. You almost got killed, and I'm afraid that if you're around me, you'll still be hurt, and I don't want that. You just stay in Texas where you're safe."

"No, Dallas, I'm coming home."

"Stay there. This isn't your home."

"Well, I'm coming anyway."

"Please, Shay, don't make this any harder than it already is. I have nothing for you. I'm going to sign the ranch away, and most of the cattle are in the mortgage too. I've already told most of the guys that their job will be done the end of the month. They said they're all staying as long as I need them."

"Are you saying that I am not welcome if I do come?"

"Oh, Shay, I want you so bad, but I have nothing to give you. Good-bye, darling." He was crying, and the line went dead.

Shay dialed the ranch again.

"Hello, Z bar 3."

"Martha, this is Shay again. I know Dallas is going through a bad time right now. He told me not to come back. I wanted you to know I am coming back no matter what. Don't let anything happen to him until I get there. Don't tell him I'm coming."

"Okay, Mr. Glen, I'll tell Hank you can work on the car tomorrow."

"Thanks, Martha; I'll see you in a day or two. Good-bye."

"Ten o'clock. Okay, that will be fine. Good-bye."

Martha hung up the phone just as Dallas walked in and poured himself a cup of coffee.

"What's wrong with the car?"

"I don't know. The check engine light is on or something," Martha lied and hurried off to tell Hank to keep their stories straight.

Shay's mom walked into the great room where Shay was sitting just as she hung up the phone.

"I don't want to rush off, but I'm going home just as soon as I can get a flight out of here. Dallas needs me."

"Oh, darling, do you have to go so soon? It seems like you just got here."

"I'll come back real soon, and I'll bring Dallas with me."

"Does he really mean that much to you?"

"Yes, Mom, he's very special. I've never met a man like him. I know you and Dad will really like him."

"Are you talking about this Dallas," said her father who was standing in the doorway, listening.

"Yes."

"Do you love him?"

"Yes, very much."

"So you are going to get married?"

"I don't know. He told me to stay in Texas because he doesn't have anything to offer me. He's such a proud man. But he's a Christian, and he's honest, trustworthy, protective of me, steadfast, and hardworking, but he would never ask me to marry him until he could give me everything he thinks my heart desires. He can't get it through his thick head. The only thing I want is him. He doesn't think he's good enough for me unless he can give me all these things." Shay started to cry. They talked far into the night, and when she went to bed, she had a smile on her face and a peace in her heart. "All things work together for good to them that love God."

CHAPTER TWENTY-ONE

Dallas was more down in the dumps then he had ever been in his half-long life as he sat on top of Boulder Butte and thought about the last several months. He had ridden past the hay fields that were brown and dried up into the bluff country where they pastured cattle. On past dried-up ponds behind dams that he and his dad had built so they could water the cattle, up to the top of one of the highest buttes on that part of the ranch. From here, he could see for miles in every direction. He saw a few cattle here and there, most of them hidden from sight behind a hill or down in a ravine. He was going to miss the ranch, and he didn't know what was in store for him, but one thing he did know was God said in his word in Romans 8:28, "And we know that all things work together for good to them that love God." He believed it. Why did he believe it? First of all, he had always believed it, and now it came down to the fact that this was the only thing he had left to believe in.

He circled back to the east until he came to the river and followed it north. He passed between the Missouri and the homestead on up about half a mile to the original place where his great-great-grandfather first built. There was the old one-room house and small barn. This wasn't the one that Austin built, but Dallas and his dad had built it as close to the original one as they could. He pushed on farther north and finally stopped on the top of another butte to eat the lunch that Martha had sent with him.

It was going to be hard to see Hank and Martha and the few cowhands that were left on the ranch go find other work. Hank and Martha had been there ever since he could remember. They were more like family than they were foremen. Most of the cowhands had been on the ranch for several years. He had already let the latecomers go when things got tough and money got short. He sure didn't want to do that because they still had about the same amount of stock to take care of, but everybody dug in, and somehow they managed to get all the work done. He sat there on the ground overlooking the ranch to the south, eating a fried chicken drumstick. Martha was never satisfied to just send a sandwich or two. No, she had to send fried chicken. There was even a piece of cherry pie in the lunch, which he had eaten first.

Dallas had had big plans for the Z bar 3. He could see some day having a Christian dude ranch where fathers and their sons or families could come and enjoy this wonderful country and become close to the land, one another, and God. That would never happen. This was all his, he thought as he took in the sight of the ranch from the top of the world, at least for a few more days. He had done his best. There was no more that he could do. When the cattle prices went down, what little money came in he had to use to buy feed for the cattle because without rain, there was no grass on the entire ranch. Then he had to deal with the sick and dying cattle and the prairie fires. It was more than he could handle. He even had to sell some of the horses and cattle to buy feed for the rest of the herd. There was no money to pay on the note because of those twenty thousand acres that they hadn't needed in the first place. He just wished his father hadn't mortgaged the whole ranch. He thought of that verse over in Proverbs, "Trust in the Lord with all thine heart and lean not on thy own understanding. In all thy ways acknowledge him, and he will direct thy path." He sure didn't know what God had planned for him, but he was still going to trust him.

Off to the east and as far as he could see to the south, the Missouri River glistened in the noonday sun. It was beautiful. Off to the west, far in the distance, he could see the main gate to the ranch with its stone pillars and steel wagon wheel gates, and laid out before him were the ranch buildings. Behind that, he could see the tarred airstrip his dad just had to have.

He thought of the history of the ranch. His great-great-grandfather coming up from Texas with a few cattle, driving them day after day because he didn't have the money to send them on the railroad like the big operators did. The railroad unloaded hundreds of cattle on the east side of the river opposite what was called the strip. The strip was a section of land several miles wide between the Indian reservations leading to the grassland farther west. The big operators were all gone, and now the Z bar 3 was one of the biggest ranches in the whole state. He thought of all the hard work that had gone into the ranch in the last hundred plus years, but it had come to the end of the line. After next week, it would all belong to somebody else.

He hated to leave this place, this was all he knew. He had gone away to college and even a couple of mission trips to South America, but he always came back. He never thought the day would come when he would ever leave the ranch for good. He had dreamed of the day he would find the right girl for a wife, and together they would raise their family here. Then one of his sons would someday take over the ranch, just like he did and his father before him and his father's father before him. He had dreamed that Shay might be that woman, but that dream had been dashed to the ground just like all of the others.

Off to the south, Dallas spotted what he thought was an airplane, and he watched it come right up the river. What in the world was it? It must be some kind of military jet or a fighter or something probably out of Sioux Falls. No . . . it was white and coming straight up the river like crazy. He was low as he screamed over where Dallas was sitting in what little grass was still on the ranch as he pulled it into a 90-degree bank and made a complete circle of the ranch. Dallas didn't know who it was, but that pilot was flying that plane like a fighter. When he went over the second time, he had slowed down a bit and he was so low that Dallas could see a couple notches of flaps come down. He made a slow turn to the west and came in over the runway not more than a hundred feet off the ground. It looked to Dallas that he was dragging the airstrip. That's pilot talk for looking over a runway to see what condition it is in. As he pulled up off the east end, he gave it full power and climbed up to about eight hundred feet, and Dallas watched as the Lear came around again. He was slower now, and just as he came over the butte that Dallas was sitting on, the wheels came down. "That *fool* is going to land," Dallas said to himself.

Only a couple of times had jets landed on their airstrip. Once when the governor of North Dakota was there and once when some big horse buyer from Texas flew in. He had made five or six passes at it before he finally landed. His dad had said maybe we will have to shoot him down. Dallas watched as that big white bird turned onto final approach. This guy knew what he was doing. He was low and slow and his wheels kissed the runway just after he crossed the threshold. He rolled to the other end of the airstrip and turned around like he was going to take off again, but he didn't. Had the bank sent a buyer even before he had signed the papers? The least they could do was to wait until he was gone. Dallas watched as he saw Hank's pickup race toward the airstrip in flying dust and stop just short of the plane.

Hank wondered what was going on, and he wasn't going to take any chances after some of the things that had happened in the last few weeks. He stopped where he could see the door, and as he got out of the truck, he took his 30-30 Winchester from off the rifle rack behind the seat. He stood behind the hood of the truck as he watched the door open and the stairway come down. A man descended the stairs carrying two bags and set them on the ground and turned and helped a woman down the steps. When she looked up, Hank recognized Shay.

What a beautiful woman, Hank thought. *She's almost as pretty as my Martha.* Hank threw the rifle in on the seat and hurried over to the plane. "Shay, it's so good to see you! I knew you were an angel, but I didn't expect you to fly in on a white bird." The pilot looked at Hank and grinned.

"Hank, this is Steve, the best pilot in North America. Steve, this is Hank the ranch foreman."

"Good to meet you, Hank. You be a good girl, Shay, or I'll have to come back and get you," said the pilot as he climbed back into the plane.

Dallas watched what was going on from his perch on Boulder Butte. He watched as Hank and one other person walked back to the pickup and the plane started rolling to the other end of the runway. He turned around and gave it full power, and halfway down the airstrip, the plane broke ground, the wheels came up, and the plane shot out over the river. Dallas watched as he went out about two miles and turned around and came in not more than three hundred feet over the buildings. He must have been doing close to five hundred miles an hour. Just as he went over the house, he pulled it up, and he climbed like an eagle. Dallas stood there and watched as the jet disappeared into the western sky.

"Man, am I glad you're here," said Hank, "Dallas is having a real rough time. He told me this morning that he was going to sign the ranch away in the next few days. He needs you now more than he has ever needed anybody in his life."

"Does Dallas think that, or is that your idea?"

"Oh, he knows that even though he may not admit it."

"Where is he?"

"He left this morning to ride one last time around the ranch. Martha packed him a lunch because he said he would be gone most of the day. I saw him ride between the river and the buildings a couple of hours ago, and I would guess he was probably up on top of Boulder Butte when you flew in. I've been keeping an eye on him the last few days because I knew how low he was. You go get rid of those fancy city clothes, and I'll saddle Midnight for you.

"Thanks, Hank. You're way too good to me."

"Well, if you're going to be my daughter-in-law, I better start being good to you. I guess not really my daughter-in-law, but in my heart you will be."

Shay reached over and kissed Hank on the cheek. "That's the nicest thing anybody has ever said to me."

Martha was standing on the front porch when they pulled up, and the minute she saw it was Shay, she came running to the truck.

"Oh, darling, it is so good to have you back," said Martha as she threw her arms around Shay. "Come in the house. I want to hear all about your trip to Texas."

"No, Martha, I'm going to change clothes and go and find Dallas."

"Oh yes, I understand. How long are you staying?"

"I am home to stay if Dallas will let me."

"If he won't let you, we'll kick him out," she said with a smile. "He really needs you right now."

By the time she had her clothes changed, Hank was back with Midnight. Even the horse seemed glad to see her.

After the plane was out of sight, Dallas sat back down on the ground, wondering who could that be who got off the plane. Well, Hank was there. He could handle it, and it really didn't make any difference to him. He had nothing to do with the ranch anyway. If it was a buyer, let him have it.

He could just make out one lone rider coming around the end of the barn and head in his direction. It was probably Hank looking for him. He thought he should get up and go see what he wanted, but he really didn't care. As the rider got closer, he realized it wasn't Hank. It must be Pedro as small as the rider was. He lay back in the grass and watched the clouds float by. The rider was closer now, and then he looked again. It wasn't Pedro. It was Shay! He waited as she rode up to him.

"What are you doing here?" he asked in a gruff voice.

"Well, hello to you too," she said with a smile.

"I thought I told you not to come."

"Since when did I do what you told me to?"

"Shay, there's nothing here for you. In fact, there's nothing here for me. I've failed. Soon the ranch will belong to someone else."

"What happened to all things work together for good to them that love God?"

"I still believe it," he said, "but I have to admit it doesn't look to good right now. Evidently, this ranch is not what God wants for me."

"How about us?"

"Yeah, us too."

"Would you like to keep the ranch," she asked.

"Sure," he replied

"Can I ask you a question?"

"I guess so."

Shay got down on one knee. "Will you marry me?"

"Shay, I would like to, but I have nothing to give you."

"I don't want anything. I just want you."

"But I have no way to support you."

"Would you agree to marry me if you had the ranch?"

"Sure, because then, I could offer you a home and some means of support. Someday I will be able to do that again, but not yet."

"Okay, let me get this straight. If it wasn't that you had to give up the ranch and you still had it, then you would marry me?"

"Yes, I want to be able to take care of you in the way you should be taken care of."

"I got you!" she said as she threw down a piece of paper in his lap.

"What's this?"

"That, my dear boy, is my half of the ranch. Now marry me or get off my land."

Dallas picked up the piece of paper and opened it. After several minutes of looking at it, he said, "This is a mortgage release."

"Yes, I know. It cost me two and a half million."

"How did you get it?"

"The bank was glad to sell it."

"No, I mean, where did you get the money?"

"Daddy gave it to me as part of my inheritance."

"Your dad has that kind of money? I thought you said he was in real estate?"

"He is. He owns some land in Texas."

"Man, how much land does he own?"

"I don't know for sure, but I think about forty acres."

"Does he call that a ranch?"

"No, they call it downtown Houston."

"What?"

"He owns a lot of the Houston skyline."

"What do you mean?"

"You country boys don't know anything. When you look at a city and see all of the tall buildings, they call that the skyline."

"Yes, I know that," said Dallas, "but what do you mean he owns the skyline?"

"Daddy owns a lot of the buildings in downtown Houston."

Dallas just sat and looked at Shay with a puzzled look on his face.

"Why would your father let you put two and a half million in a ranch that he's never seen with a guy he doesn't know? He must be crazy."

"He is. He's crazy about me. When I told him about you, he asked if I was going to marry you, and I told him you wouldn't ask me without asking him first. I told him how protective you were of me and what a good Christian you are. Besides, I told him I loved you and wanted to marry you, but you were too proud to ask me until you knew you could give me all of the dumb things you think I need. I don't need things, Dallas. I only need you. He liked you without ever meeting you."

"Shay, I can't let you do this."

"It's too late. I already have."

"But, Shay, it's not fair that you have to buy into the ranch."

"Oh, so you were going to ask me to marry you but then have me sign a palimony agreement so what was yours was yours and none of it was mine?"

"Don't be silly, Shay, I would never do that."

"Neither would I. What's mine is yours. Two and a half million is just a drop in the bucket from what my inheritance really is, and no, you aren't marrying me for my money. You didn't know I had any money when you agreed to marry me. You thought I was just some unemployed gal from Rapid City."

"Whose jet was that that you came in?"

"That was Daddy's jet, and he's sending it back in a week to get us to come to Texas."

Dallas just shook his head. "This is crazy."

"No, it is all things work together for good."

"So are you going to marry me, or do I have to get somebody to throw you off my land?"

"Wait a minute, doll. Don't get pushy. I still own the land. Either you marry me, or I'll have you arrested for trespassing," said Dallas.

"Oh, don't do that, sir. I'll marry you!" She came into his arms, and they rolled in the grass in a passionate kiss.

After several minutes, Dallas stood up and said, "I have something for you." He opened up his saddlebag and took out a miniature cowboy hat and gave it to Shay.

She turned it over several times and laid it in the palm of her hand and said, "That's so cute, I'll keep it forever to remember this day by."

"Open it."

"Open what?"

"Lift off the top."

She did and then started to cry. "Oh, Dallas, oh, Dallas, I love you so much." Inside the little hat on a bed of red velvet was the most beautiful diamond she had ever seen. "When did you get this?" she asked.

"Several weeks ago, I was waiting for all the things."

She was in his arms again, "Here put it on for me."

"No," said Dallas

"Why not?"

"Remember we have to talk to Daddy first."

"Oh, that's silly."

"No, it isn't, but you can wear it until we go to Houston. Just don't let him see it."

CHAPTER TWENTY-TWO

The next morning, Shay helped Martha get breakfast, but Martha didn't notice the rock on Shay's finger. Shay was on cloud nine and couldn't wait to tell somebody. Dallas came into the kitchen and said, "What smells so good?" as he poured himself a cup of coffee.

"Martha has fresh caramel rolls," answered Shay, and she mouthed, "I love you." He sat down at the table and couldn't stop smiling. The Lord was so good as he remembered "all things work together."

"Now what's keeping Hank? Breakfast is going to get cold."

"Where is Hank?" asked Dallas.

"He said he wanted go down to the horse barn and check on the new foal that was born late yesterday afternoon. You would think that the mother couldn't do it without him. He's such a worry wart when it comes to some of those horses."

"Well," said Dallas, "we don't want to lose a foal. We only have a hundred some horses. You never know when we might need another one."

About that time, they heard Hank's footsteps on the back porch as he brushed off his boots on the boot scraper. "Morning, folks," he said as he hung up his jacket and hat. "We sure got a nice stud colt, flashy black-and-white. Make a good ride for your son someday."

Dallas laughed and asked, "Which son?"

"You better get on the ball and have a son pretty soon. Who's going to run this ranch when you're gone?" Hank was doing his best to get Dallas to forget about the mortgage that was due.

"Hank quit talking and get washed up," Martha said. "Breakfast is getting cold."

"Sorry, dear, I'll hurry."

Shay was getting used to the big morning meals here on the ranch. She knew it set you up for the whole day of hard work. As they were sitting having one last cup of java, Dallas said, "Hank, I want you to get all the cowhands together and have them come to the house as soon as you can this morning. I need to talk to them. Have Mrs. Miller come along with Evert. Martha, I want you to sit in on the meeting too."

"Sure, Mr. Z.," she said in a glum voice.

Hank slid his chair back and stood up, "You sure you want to do this?" he asked. "Why don't you just let me tell the guys?"

"No, I need to do this."

"Okay." He left the table and headed out to give the men the message. It wasn't long before Hank came back in the house. "I found everybody. I told them to be here at ten if that's okay."

"That's just fine. You're a good man, Hank. Shay, can I see you in the office?"

"Sure, I'll be right there." She hung up the towel she had in her hand and took off her apron. She followed Dallas into the office, and they closed the door. Dallas took Shay in his arms and smothered her with kisses. "This is going to be fun," he said.

"I know it," Shay responded in between kisses. "I could hardly keep from hollering at Martha to look at my ring!" They hugged and kissed some more.

"I feel so sorry for Dallas," said Hank. "He's done everything he knows how to do to save the ranch. With the cattle prices the way they are and no rain, it was just too much."

"I know it," said Martha. "What will we do?"

"I'm not too worried. We have a good heavenly Father."

About ten minutes to ten, the first cowboy arrived. "I guess this is it," he said as he hung up his hat on one of the pegs by the door. It wasn't long until the rest of them filtered in. Most of them had a sullen look on their face, and there wasn't the joking and laughing like there usually would have been. The Millers were the last to arrive, and you could tell that Edith had been crying. At ten o'clock sharp, the door to the office opened, and Shay walked out, followed by Dallas. Shay went over and stood in the kitchen door with Martha who put her arm around her and whispered, "I'm sorry, dear." Shay just smiled.

What a brave child, Martha thought. She knew how much Shay loved Dallas and how good their life could have been here on the ranch. Now she wasn't sure just what they would do.

"Thanks for coming," Dallas started. "As most of you know, we've had some hard times here on the ranch the last several months. You know that we've had a big mortgage hanging over our heads, and with the cattle prices and no rain, it's been very difficult to keep up with the payments. The reason I called you all here today is because I wanted to tell you myself what I've decided to do." Mrs. Miller wiped tears out of her eyes. "First of all, I want to fill you in on what's been going on around here. I talked to the sheriff this morning, and he informed me that they've made several arrests in the last couple of days. They got the ones who shot the cattle and also the two guys who started the fire. Not only that, they found out who it was who wanted to buy the ranch and where the money was coming from. It appears some people from California were in the drug business and had a lot of money that they needed to launder. Also, they planned to use the ranch and the airstrip to service their drug dealers in this part of the country. Not only did they arrest the people in California, but they also arrested Jippem from Rapid City. Second, I need all of you to stay on at the Z bar 3, and you'll see why when I tell you my plan." Cowboys looked at each other with puzzled looks on their faces. "Third, I've ordered ten semi-loads of hay from Sam Johnson. He was the guy who brought hay after the fire. Fourth, we need to build the Millers a new house. I'm sure they want to get back to their own place. Fifth, we're going to build at least ten cabins so we can get you men out of the bunkhouse and into your own quarters. We'll use the bunkhouse for part-time men. And sixth, we're going to get to work and make the Z bar 3 the best ranch in South Dakota." No one spoke and everyone sat with an unbelievable look on their face. "Any questions?"

Hank stood up and asked, "What about the mortgage?"

"Oh yeah, maybe I should mention that. It's no longer a problem. I was forced to take on a partner, and at the present time, I own fifty percent of the ranch, not one hundred percent."

"I'm not sure that was wise," said Hank. "I for one, and I think the rest of the men will agree, we would like to meet the new partner before we say if we'll stay on or not. You've been so good to all of us. I can't imagine working for anyone else."

"That's no more than fair, Hank. Shay, will you tell my new partner to come in please?"

"Sure." Everybody watched as she walked into the kitchen toward the back door. She took her hat off the peg and opened the back door. She stepped out, closing the door behind her. Every eye in the room was on the door. They waited. The door opened, and Shay walked back into the room. She came up to Dallas and whispered, "I love you," in his ear as everybody looked on and wondered what she told him. She turned around and looked at the crew who watched with blank looks on their faces. Dallas reached up and put his arm around Shay and said, "Boys, I would like you to meet my new partner. She paid off the mortgage and now owns half of the ranch. She told me to either marry her or get off her land. I had no choice. I had no other place to go."

"Don't you feel sorry for him?" asked Shay as she looked up and winked at Dallas. There was stunned silence. No one knew if they had heard right or not. Rusty raised his hand.

"Yes, Rusty, do you have a question?"

"Did I hear you right? Are you and Shay getting married?"

"Yes, Rusty, that's correct. We are getting married and will be equal partners in Z bar 3."

"Then I would like to make a statement. If Shay is the new partner, I'm staying."

"Maria and I are staying too!" chimed in Pedro.

"So am I!" hollered one cowboy after another, and before they knew it, they were surrounded by the whole crowd. They were all congratulating them, and of course, the girls wanted to see Shay's diamond.

"When is the wedding?" Martha asked.

"We haven't talked about that yet," said Dallas. "I still have to ask Shay's dad. He might say no."

"Not if I have anything to say about it. Besides, I have Daddy wound around my little finger. What Shay wants Shay gets!" Everybody was laughing, talking and laughing some more.

Martha put on some coffee and brought out the cake and cookies she had on hand, and the glum meeting turned into a party.

Later, much later when the cowboys all left, they were in much better spirits than when they came in. They all thought they were going to be without a job, and now it looked better than ever. Martha looked at

Shay without a smile and said, "You haven't asked me if you could have Dallas."

Had she hurt Martha? Shay wondered. "Will you give your little boy to me in marriage?"

"Yes, yes!" she screamed as she took Shay in her arms. "Please, please take him off my hands."

"Not so fast," said Dallas. "You and Hank have to stay here and take care of the two of us."

"We will," they both said as they all embraced each other.

"But remember, this is not official until we go to Texas and make sure it's all right with Shay's mom and dad. It might be that we're only in business together without being married." And Dallas grinned at Shay.

"When are you going to Texas?" asked Hank.

"Probably next week," said Dallas.

"We are not," said Shay. "I told mom last night that I wasn't coming back to Texas. If they wanted to see me, they were going to have to come up here. Besides meeting you, Dallas, I want them to meet Martha and Hank and the rest of the guys as well as seeing the ranch."

Two days later, as they were having a cup of coffee, they heard the scream of a jet going over the house. By the time they got out on the front porch, the Lear was making the turn onto the final approach. Before Shay and Dallas got to the airstrip, the pilot was just shutting down the engines.

"Are you nervous?" asked Shay.

"No, these have to be very nice people to have a daughter as wonderful as you." He gave her a hug. Dallas and Shay walked closer as her mother and father got out of the plane.

Shay ran to them and hugged them and said, "I'm so glad you came! I know you're going to love Z bar 3. Mom and Daddy, I want you to meet Dallas, the most wonderful man in the world."

Dallas put out his hand to Mrs. Everhart, but she ignored it and threw her arms around him. "If you're half as good as Shay says you are, you truly are wonderful."

"I sure can tell where Shay gets her beauty," Dallas said.

"Oh, you are so sly! I like you already."

"And you, sir, it's good to have you at the ranch," said Dallas as he took Shay's Daddy's hand. "I need to talk to you."

"No need, I gave my answer to your unasked question when Shay and I talked in Houston. You have mine and her mother's blessing. She told us what a man of God you were, and I knew then she had found the right man. I'll tell you right now—Shay always gets what she wants."

"Thank you, Daddy! I know you'll like Dallas a lot, the more you get to know him. He said I couldn't wear my ring until he asked you if he could marry me, but I talked him out of it."

"See what I mean?" said Mr. Everhart. "She always gets what she wants."

"Come, let's go to the house. I should be helping Martha with dinner. She's such a precious woman. Steve, you and Bryan come too. Daddy will surely let you eat before you go back. Dinner on the ranch is the best meal of the day."

As they walked into the house, Hank was still sitting at the table with a cup of coffee in his hand, and Martha was standing at the range.

"Martha, get over here," said Shay. "I want you to meet Mom and Daddy.

"Mom and Dad, this is Martha, Dallas's adopted mother and Hank, his father."

"Not really," said Hank, "he has to pay us to be his folks." They all laughed.

"What can I help with?" asked Shay.

"Go ahead and set the table," Martha said.

"What can I do?" asked Shay's mother.

"You just sit and watch Shay to make sure she does it right," said Martha with a grin.

"Come on, Hank. Join us in the great room."

"No, I better go down to the barn and check on Music. She foaled an hour ago. A nice black-and-white filly."

Dallas and Mr. Everhart talked and got to know each other while the women did the same in the kitchen. They had been together only a few minutes, but they already felt at home.

"My, you didn't have to put on a Thanksgiving feed like this! We're not used to such a thing." said Shay's mother.

"Don't tell them that. We kind of like it,' said Hank.

"You might just as well get used to it, Mother. This isn't a special meal. This is how Martha always cooks. You should see the feed she puts on when the guys are here for branding. Most of the guys would come and work for nothing just so they could eat Martha's cooking."

"Your daughter is getting pretty good at it too. She's a lot of help around here."

"I've never seen such a house! When I saw it from the air; I thought it was a lodge or something. It's so warm and cozy, just like I would imagine in a Western movie."

"Wait until you see the bedrooms," said Shay. "You'll fall in love with them."

After dinner, Hank got up from the table and said, "I'll help Martha with the dishes. Why don't you take a drive and show them around the ranch."

"I can take a few minutes and give Martha a hand," said Shay.

"No, you go and show your mom and dad the ranch. I know they would like that."

The four of them got in the four-wheel-drive four-door Ford and started off on some of the back roads of the ranch. They headed past the original homestead and cemetery down to the river boat landing, heading south following the river to the high bluff.

"This is the place I always thought would be a good place for a Christian dude ranch," Dallas said, "a place where men and their sons could come to get closer together, enjoying the land and slower pace of ranch life and getting to know God better."

"That's a great idea," said Mr. Everhart. "I'll have to bring Pastor Joel up here to see this beautiful place. Who knows maybe the three of us could work something out?" They continued to drive for the next couple of hours and finally returned to the ranch house. The sun was just setting in the west when they pulled up to the front porch.

"I'll bet you guys are tired. It's been a long day. Why don't I show you to your room? You can get a good night's sleep. Tomorrow will be a full day of making wedding plans."

Shay's Dad and Dallas stopped in the kitchen for a night snack, and Shay took her mother upstairs to their room. When she walked in, she stopped so fast that Shay ran right into her.

"Shay, this is wonderful! What a beautiful guest room. Look at that canopy bed and the patchwork comforter. I've never seen a log bed like that. And the river glowing in the moonlight makes me see why you fell in love with this place."

"In here is the bathroom, Mom, and you can hang your things in this walk-in closet."

"What a guest room!"

"There are three more just like this one. I'm sleeping in one, and there are two empty ones."

"How big is this house anyway?"

"It's big. I'll show you around in the morning."

Later, much later, after Shay's folks were in bed, Shay and Dallas sat in the great room, talking over the day.

"I really like your folks, Shay. They are so kind and just plain ordinary. I know a lot of people with money, and you can't stand them."

"Mom said that she and Dad really like you too."

"I suppose your mother probably has the wedding all planned."

"No, she'll offer some suggestions, but she won't tell me what to do. I want to get married here at the ranch. This is where we're going to start our life together, with this land and these people. Oh, we'll have to have a reception in Houston for the folks' benefit, but when I was home, we had no church connection."

"Are you sure that's what you want? I'll do anything to make you happy."

"Just marrying me makes me happy," she said, kissing him.

By the time the folks left, all the wedding plans were made, and they were treating Dallas like he was their son instead of their future son-in-law. Dallas and Shay stood and watched the jet lift off the end of the runway and head south. With arms around each other, they watched until the plane disappeared into the solid overcast. A flash of lightning and a clap of thunder and it started to rain, light at first, then it grew heavier. Leaving the truck they had come in, Dallas took Shay by the hand and started walking toward the ranch house. By the time they got there, it was pouring, and they were soaking wet. "And we know that all things work together for good to them that love God," Dallas said, and he took Shay in his arms and kissed her passionately as the rain soaked them and the thirsty ground.

THE END